HEAVEN SENT

Paisley Jacobs

WHISPERS OF VICE AND VIRTUE SERIES

This is a work of fiction. Names, characters, places, and incidents are products of the author's imagination are used fictitiously, and are not to be constructed as real. Any resemblance to actual events, locales, organizations, or persons living or dead, is entirely coincidental.

ACKNOWLEDGEMENTS

To those who never stopped believing in me. I couldn't have done this without you.

To Vance, my partner, my biggest supporter, and the one who believed in me the most, thank you from the bottom of my heart.

CONTENT WARNINGS

Choking/Breath Play

Physical Abuse

Murder

Kidnapping

Torture

Parental Neglect

Violence

Mentions of Rape and Incest

PLAYLISTS

Scan to listen or
Find at Paisley_Jacobs on Spotify

Nicolai & Angelina

Playlist

Mafia Training

Playlist

Whispers of Vice and Virtue

Playlist

To all the sweet little angels who can't keep their eyes off the devil. This one's for you.

CHAPTER 1

Angelina

I'm lying on my bed in my pink room, deep in my thoughts. Looking around, it feels like I'm living in someone else's room. Pink is not even my favorite color, but my opinion didn't matter when my parents picked the paint; my opinion never mattered. My closet to the side is full of jeans without holes, long dresses, jackets, and absolutely nothing that does my body any favors. A chandelier sits above me, with light shining through the sheer white canopy surrounding my bed. A white desk sits in the corner; otherwise, my room is empty. Lifeless. I'm sick of feeling caged in, so for once in my life, I let my intrusive thoughts take over and think up a plan to get out of this hell hole of a home.

Never in my life would I have thought I'd resort to stealing money, but desperate times lead to desperate measures.

I'm drowning in my father's grasp, and it's not like my mother can help when she's too busy drowning in his riches. The only way out is to leave, but I don't have money for a hotel, let alone to survive on my own. My father gives my mother all the money in the world, but none to me. When I say he wants me locked away forever, I mean that. I can barely have friends, go anywhere alone, and God forbid if I were to get a boyfriend. I'm convinced my father would have a stroke if I even mentioned the idea. He is always working, and my mother is always out spending. I don't think I've ever sat down and had dinner with both present. My entire life has been so lonely I can't take it anymore.

Ten years ago

"Mommy, can I please have a baby sister? Or even a brother! I'll do anything! The laundry, dishes, anything!" My

mother dropped the plate she was holding, and it shattered. She stared at me like she had seen a ghost. "Momma?"

My father heard what I had asked, walked up to my mother, put a hand on her shoulder, and said, "Honey, you weren't even supposed to be born. In fact, you almost weren't, but Victoria here is a fighter."

My mother laughed it off and said, "Baby, don't listen to your father; he's just joking. But mommy can't have any more kids. So, no." That was the end of that conversation. I never mentioned it again.

That night, I heard so much fighting. My parents fight constantly, and when they do, I put my headphones on to tune it out. All I wanted was a sibling to play with. Sometimes, their disagreements get physical, but my mother has always been good at hiding the aftermath from the public eye.

My father has never laid a hand on me, but that's not to say he hasn't raised his voice or looked at me with pure hatred in his eyes. He cares more about controlling me than my well-being. It's like he wants me to be his lap dog, listen to his every command, and live solely for him. I don't think he wanted me or any children at all, but here I am, and this is his way of dealing with it. To this day, I don't understand why he is the way he is. I've asked him why I can't leave, why he doesn't like me having friends, and why he hurts my mom. I have asked him every question I can think of for years, and every time I do, he gets angry and calls me ungrateful. I've given up on asking questions, knowing I'll never get the answers I so desperately want.

Leaving my mom with my father seems heartless, but she wouldn't come with me even if I offered—she'd rat me out. She's too scared of what would happen if she got caught. I mean this kindly; my mother is not brave. When it comes to my father, she is scared, weak, and helpless. Some may say I am, too, considering I've done nothing to stop him. But how could I? He's stronger and wiser than me, and I have no money to get help. My mother is gone quite often and always comes back with her arms full of shopping bags. I'm certain that half of the things she owns still have tags on them, collecting dust. I don't know why she shops so much; she doesn't need any of it. To be honest, if I could leave as often as she does and avoid my father, I'd probably do the same thing. This house suffocates the air out of you, sometimes literally with my father's hands around my mother's neck.

I love my mom, and I don't resent her like I do my father, but she's shut herself out of my life and made me even lonelier. I know she cares about me, but she ends up with bruises whenever she shows it. As a kid, spending time with my mom always ended up making messes whether in the kitchen, with toys, or even accidents. It's normal for kids to make a mess, but if I did, it got my mom into trouble. It got to the point where she couldn't take the abuse that came with mother-daughter time. Nowadays, she hardly speaks to me; she's never home, and there are very few motherly moments I can recall. She's been more of a glorified roommate than a parent. It hurts, but I'm used to it by now. Unlike her, I will not sit around any longer with their arguments and fatherly control devouring me whole. I turned eighteen last month; it's time they started treating me like an adult.

I plan on leaving my parents tonight. I texted my only friends, Ginevra and Rosanna, and got them on board. I asked Rosanna to bring me a few things, a slutty dress, makeup, and heels. I don't own any dresses that show off my body; I have very little makeup and absolutely no heels. On the bright side, I stole my mom's curling iron and was able to do my hair before they picked me up.

Rosanna and Gia are my girls, and I can't tell you how many times my father tried to remove them from my life. Eventually, he learned he couldn't scare them off, and they weren't going anywhere. I love them so much for staying with me through thick and thin. I hardly ever get to see them, but that doesn't stop them from being here for me.

I met them both in town with my father once. I'm not allowed to go out, but he lets me leave a few times if he's alongside me. All three of us immediately clicked, and I got their numbers while my father wasn't looking. We've been best friends ever since.

Rosanna is kind of like the mom of the group. I usually call her Rosie. She's responsible most of the time, mature, and the smartest of us three. She still has her rebellious moments here and there, but her family pressures her to uphold a good reputation to their name.

Gia is different. She's the best part of us three, the brightest. She's like a bubbly, pink princess; while some may find her annoying, I find her refreshing. There is so much negativity in my life, so her positive energy is exactly what I need. Her heart has broken a few times, but she doesn't let it affect her persona. That's what I love most about her. She doesn't change for anyone or hold back who she is.

They're picking me up tonight around two in the morning, typically when my parents sleep. I've only snuck out a few times. Luckily, I have yet to be caught.

I pack up my clothes, toiletries, makeup, and everything else so they're ready when I get home later. All of it only fills two duffel bags, so I hide the bags under my bed for the time being. It doesn't feel like I'm running away; it feels more like finally getting the freedom I deserve. I'm excited but nervous. I love leaving the house, but I fear getting caught.

My friends are parking a few blocks away when they get here, so I'll have to walk because my father's security would undoubtedly notice their headlights in the driveway. The cameras pick up on lights but not movements at night. It's so dark outside that it won't catch me sneaking out. I have a security guard outside my door every night, but he's under strict orders not to enter my room without my father's permission. I guess they didn't think to put one outside my window.

At ten to two, I started climbing down the lattice outside my window and walking toward my friend's car. Being alone in the dark is scary, but I love a good thrill. I crave the adrenaline rush that comes with sneaking out.

Eventually, I see Gia's white Mercedes in the distance. I speed-walk to the car and hop in. Both girls are squealing, of course. It's been so long since I've seen them, and I missed their faces.

I lean over the center console and look at Rosie with hopeful eyes. "Did you bring it?" I ask her.

She gives me a look as if she'd ever let me down. "Duh! What would you do without me?"

Rosie passes me a bag full of necessities. She's a lifesaver because I wouldn't have had anything to wear. I blame my father for that. I asked her to bring a slutty dress, and of course, she brought the skimpiest she owned. I remove my sweatpants and tee shirt and change into the dress. It's a black strappy one that stops right below my ass. I can barely keep it from covering myself when I'm sitting down. I dig in the bag for the tall high heels and slide those on my feet. I can tell these are going to be painful, but beauty is pain.

I do some quick facial makeup and then mascara to make my mahogany brown eyes pop. Lastly, I add red lipstick, my favorite color. Once I'm finished, I do a quick look over and smile. I think I look hot, which is what I'm going for. I've got to be alluring and easy on the eyes if I'm going to accomplish tonight's goal.

If I'm going to be a gold digger for the night, I have to look the part; at least, that's the excuse I tell myself for wearing this dress. Underneath all the excuses, I know that I love how I look. I look like a confident virgin slut, the best side of me.

"Finished! Rosie, I owe you one."

Both of my friends look me up and down.

"OMG, Girl, you are hot shit," Gia says as she makes her way onto the main road.

Rosie motions with her hands at the dress and says, "Yeah, there's no way you won't get any man you want like that."

La Citta del Peccato is the most exclusive club in all of Italy. I've never tried to get in, so today will be my first attempt. The club is based in Milan, the city where I live, and one of the wealthiest cities in Italy. It's a beautiful city, and being outside feels more like home than the house I grew up in. Lights cover the streets, Vespas everywhere you look, and bakeries around every corner with some of the best croissants I've ever had. Every time I ride with the girls I put the window down, cross my arms on the windowsill, and lean my head down, admiring the city. It should be a crime to keep someone from the beauty of it.

Access is the only flaw in our plan, but we will try our best to get in. Only the richest of the rich are allowed access. Most people call this place a nightclub, but it requires a membership card to get in, and that monthly fee costs an arm and a leg.

Your millionaire-stupid-rich if you're here, and that's precisely why we need to get in. I'm sure my father has a membership here, but I'm not him, and he would never put my name on his guest list. Any man I steal from here will provide me with enough to get out from under my father's grasp, at least for the time being. Whether the man has cash or cards in his wallet, I'll make it work until he blocks the spending. Then I'll do it again to another man, and another, and another.

We arrive, and my nerves creep in. We are going off on a limb by flirting with the guard at the door to get in. He asks for our membership cards, so we hand him the fake ones Gia got for us. He looks at the cards, and then back at us girls about three different times, clearly not buying it. He says something into his walking talkie so quietly that I can't hear it. All three of us just kind of stand here awkwardly, either waiting to get inside or get booted.

A few seconds pass until his walkie-talkie makes a sound. Surprisingly, he steps to the side and lets us in. We jump and squeal, feeling very accomplished with ourselves. But then we remember the mature audience of this club and straighten ourselves before walking in.

We walk through the doors with our shoulders held high, chin up, and radiating confidence. As soon as we're in, people are looking at us, and whispering about us. Some girls look at us with pure jealousy and malice in their eyes, but I notice a few other girls with interest in their gaze. Plenty of men are looking our way, but none catch my attention. I carry myself confidently, aware of the appreciative glances. I look around, trying my best to find the man I'll steal from, but no one has caught my eye yet.

CHAPTER 2

Nicolai

The bouncer interrupts my train of thought as his voice rings through the walkie-talkie sitting on my desk. "Sir some girls here with fakes are trying to get in. What do you want me to do with them?"

Typically, I wouldn't allow it, but my breathing stopped after looking at the cameras. I lean in toward the cameras to get a closer look. The blonde in the middle is stunning. She has long honey-blonde hair, the body of a goddess, and a smile brighter than the sun itself. Two other attractive girls are with her, but they don't compare. I recognize the girls with her slightly, considering I know everyone in this city. But the blonde? I've never seen her, and I'm certain of it because I would have remembered her. Who is she? I contemplate letting them in for a moment but then let my bad judgment win this argument, wanting to see more of her.

I pick up my walkie and hit the talk button. "Let them in," I say.

I watch my bouncer over the cameras as he says, "Yes, sir."

They seem very satisfied with themselves after he lets them pass, and honestly, they should be. The security here is strict as fuck. I own *La Citta del Peccato*, but this isn't my main source of income; it's more like a front for what is.

I make most of my riches gambling, which I was introduced to at a very young age by my father. I was only a kid when my parents died, so I couldn't learn much since he never got the chance to teach me more.

My grandparents took me in after they passed, but they're old and tired, now and even back then. They didn't have much choice but to take me in. I don't think they ever recovered from their son being brutally murdered. When I turned eighteen, I moved out and made my way. I still talk to them and visit, but it's like keeping company with a wall.

I've spent most of my time growing up teaching myself until I could master the game. My father was the king of gambling and a highly known mafia boss. He was the best out there, which is likely what got him killed. After both my parents died, I did everything in my power to replace my father as the king of gambling and get as close as I could to the mafia by being a part of it.

However, I am careful with my gambling. My father won every game he played and never once let up. I learned from his mistakes and am willing to throw a game now and then, so I don't have a target on my back. I know for a fact that they died because of my father's job; it's just a matter of whether it was one of his fellow employees, enemies, or even just some random in a poker game. Regardless of his gambling and occupation, my father was a good person, and I will find out who killed him and get my vengeance.

It's been years since they died, and I still haven't gotten anywhere near close to finding the killer. It's aggravating. Whoever did it, covered their tracks. But I'm not giving up. I know that's not what my father would want. He would want me to find the motherfucker and torture him until he begs for mercy.

I refocus my thoughts and watch the blonde's every movement on the cameras. She walks in like she owns the place. Every man and woman in the club turns in her direction and takes her in. She and her friends are the center of attention, with bodies and faces like theirs, I'm not surprised. My phone rings, and I almost don't pick up, but it's an important call, so I do.

I don't bother wasting any time greeting him, so I

address him as soon as I accept the call. "Enzo."

He cuts straight to the point "I just spoke with Rocco; the

deal is set. You just have to sign some papers and confirm

everything. If you need me, call me."

"Yeah, yeah, I have it handled," I say.

"Good." He says nothing after that, and neither do I.

Enzo, my partner, ends the call. I sought Enzo out when I

turned eighteen, knowing he was high up in the mafia and a

friend of my parents. He offered me a position as a lower-rank

employee, and I took it. Everyone's got to start from

somewhere. Over time, I climbed my way up to partner with

undying loyalty, bloodshed, and an increase in skills necessary

for someone in this position. I'm proud of how far I've come,

and I'm sure my father would be too. Yet I can't help but feel like I'm failing him while his killer runs loose. I get out of my head when I see my office door open.

I stand up and greet Rocco Accardi with a handshake. He has a medium build, pitch-black shaggy hair, and a tattoo on his face. He's dressed in black pants, a black tee shirt, and a leather jacket. I look down to see him holding a biker helmet.

Rocco is in the mafia, known for his connections with corrupt public officials, banks, and other high-up mafia bosses. I need him on my team for smoother operations. Lately, the law has been on my ass, but they won't make any moves without proof. We talked for a few minutes to confirm the financial offer and details, and then I handed him some papers to sign to finalize everything.

While he's busy, I look over at the cameras on my computer. I spot the blonde right away, and she's moved to the dance floor. Once he's finished, I ask Rocco to join me in the

VIP lounge, and he follows. After all, it's an opportunity not many men would refuse. You have to be drowning in money to make it VIP and also a part of the mafia, considering illegal gambling takes place up here.

From this area, I can keep a closer eye on her. In the middle of the room sits a green, circular poker table full of chips, scattered hundred-dollar bills, playing cards, and men playing the game. The walls are black, and a large bulletproof window faces the dance floor. An LED light on the wall reads the name of my club, *La Citta Del Peccato*, the city of sin. I found it quite fitting. To the opposite side of the window sits a minibar. I don't trust a low-life employee with what goes on up here, so I decided to make it self-serve. The men get kicked out if they overdrink, and their VIP membership pays well enough to drink whatever they desire. I walk over and make a glass of

Jack Daniel's whisky and ice. I can easily afford an expensive beverage, but over the years, I've learned Jack is my favorite.

The VIP lounge gives the perfect view of the dance floor below. I grab an acid cigar from a table nearby. I learned to keep them stocked up here after I ran out one day and was desperate for a smoke. Then I walk over and take a seat by the edge so she can see me, and I can see her. She looks ethereal, unreal in the dim lighting of the club. I lean down, rest my arms on both my knees, and light the cigar. I inhale and release a puff of smoke, then lick my lips, savoring the cigar's sweetness and the tobacco's bitterness. *I wonder how sweet she tastes.*

She hasn't caught me staring yet, but she will. My body relaxes from the effect of the cigar. Rocco has been rambling on about something, but I haven't listened to a word he has said, too distracted by her. Eventually, he moves on to talk with the other men up here, but I remain seated where I am. I have the perfect view of her, and no way in hell am I giving that up for another man to take my place.

The blonde's dress is way too short, and the way she is dancing is not safe in a club full of extremely dangerous men. She is playing with fire, and she's going to get burnt if she keeps this up. She is in between her two friends, all three of them in sync with the song and touching. But they aren't dancing like most friends would. They're grinding on each other.

I'm so fucked.

As if she senses my eyes burning into her, she looks to the side and upright at me. I blow out a puff of smoke that I'm holding in while watching her move to the beat of the song. Every man in this club is eye-fucking her, but she only looks at me. She slowly brings her hands up her body, lifting her dress higher, and then her hands tangle in her long, wavy hair all while never breaking eye contact with me. *God, what is this woman doing to me?* My patience stretches so thin it breaks.

Fuck it.

CHAPTER 3

Angelina

This club is breathtaking, and I can see why you must be rich to get in. There are overhead lights that flash all different colors. The lights are bright, but at the same time, the club is dark. They're the only lights on, and people can still see you, but you could hide in the shadows if you tried. The bar sits to the side with bartenders, and just about every alcoholic beverage you can think of. Some tequilas on that shelf cost more than my life's worth. I order a vodka cranberry and continue looking around the room. The DJ plays music so loud that the room vibrates, but I don't mind the noise when I grew up in a house full of silence, except for my father's screaming. I pull my friends to the dance floor, wanting to have fun but also trying to attract more attention.

I look above at the VIP lounge, feeling someone's eyes burning into me. With just one glance, I know he's who I want, and who I will steal from. He has to be filthy rich and easy on the eyes too. I could choose anyone in this club, and I want him. He's devilishly handsome, and his profile speaks of power and ageless strength. He has chocolate-colored brown hair that's short on the sides and longer on top, *long enough to grab a handful and pull on*. His dark eyes are as beautiful as black satin. He has a cleanly shaved face; everything about him radiates cleanliness. It makes me want to corrupt him and dirty up his white shirt. He has a muscular build for sure, considering I can see his biceps straining against his white button-up. His rolled-up sleeves reveal tattoos underneath that cover his arms and hands. Large hands, might I add. He brings a cigar to his mouth and puffs a smoke, and at this moment, I wish it was my lips on his rather than the cigar. When my eyes roam further down his torso, I see he's wearing grey business pants. He's neatly dressed for a club, but most rich men here are. He grins when he catches me checking him out. His eyes catch mine and hold them. His stare is so intense it's burning me up, but I would gladly play with that fire.

Every man and even some women in this club are watching me and my friends now. Some people stopped dancing, and we were just about the only ones left on the floor. It probably helps that all three of us dressed accordingly. I wanted to make sure we all attracted attention. Gia waved her ginger hair and wore a tight white dress tonight. Rosie straightened her black hair and wore a white dress, too. They wanted to match, so I stood out among them in black. After all, I'm the one who needs to allure a man tonight and fool him, fool him well.

Rosie whispers in my ear, "Is it working?"

I talk to her but don't take my eyes off him. With a devious grin, I say, "Of course it is. I have him right where I want him."

I eye-fuck him while grinding with my friends, but somehow, that still isn't enough to bring him down here. While dancing, I move my hands up the side of my dress, scrunching it higher so that it's just barely covering my ass. Never once breaking eye contact. Then I move my hands up to my hair, part my red lips, and continue swaying to the music. Just as I predicted, his control snaps, and he's walking down the stairs to the dance floor.

I whisper to Rosie, "I got this from here on out. I'll find you when I'm ready."

My friends go disperse, and he comes to me right on cue. Most girls would be intimidated by his size; he's got to be at least six-four, and he doesn't miss the gym. But most girls aren't me. I'm not shy, and I can be a little cocky with my confidence. When you're caged up at home like me, your true colors show when free.

"I'll Make You Love Me" by Kat Leon starts playing over the speakers. He circles me while I dance alone, taking me in like a hunter who found his prey. Except I'm the hunter, and he's my prey; he just doesn't know it yet.

He stops circling me, and I feel him come up behind me. He puts his rough hands on my waist and pushes his front side to my backside. I can feel his hard erection pushing against my ass. I look down at his hand on me, so vascular and covered in intricate tattoos. I catch a glimpse of a deck of cards tattooed on his forearm and want to explore further, but I am too distracted by his presence to focus. I grind on him just like I did with my friends, and he groans in satisfaction. As he leans in, I smell hints of tobacco and leather. I've never once had a desire to smoke before, but God he makes me want nicotine.

He puts his lips to my ear, and it tickles. He whispers, "Do you have any idea how many people want to fuck you right now."

His voice is deep and dead sexy. His touch on my hip raises goosebumps to my skin. I move my face to the left by his lips and look up into his hungry, charcoal-colored eyes.

"I only want you," I say.

He again presses his lips to my ear and the contact makes me shiver.

"Good girl," he whispers.

I never thought two words could affect me so much, yet being called a good girl does things to me I'd rather not confess.

I may be soaked underneath my dress, but that doesn't mean I'll submit to him and lose track of what I came for. But would it hurt to enjoy myself a little first?

I grab his right hand and place it on my thigh, right below the hem of my dress. Then, I move my hand up to the back of his neck. He doesn't look like someone who would ask permission, but I nudge him in the right direction anyway.

I plead. "Touch me."

After he came up to me, most people went back on the dance floor seeing I was now off the table for grabs. No one here would have the guts to take me from a man like him. We're surrounded by others' backs to us and have all the privacy we need. He moves his hand up further, then stops when he realizes I'm not wearing any panties. He groans and tightens his hand on my hips and thigh to a bruising grip.

"You're killing me," he says while looking at me with lustful eyes.

He feels how wet I am and slowly pushes a finger in, then two. His breathing grows ragged, and my moans slip free.

He looks around the room. "If anyone but me looks at you right now, I will murder them cold-blooded."

I have a feeling he doesn't bluff, and that should scare me, but if anything, it turns me on more. He moves at a faster pace, and I grind on his hand and erection. It's all too much, with the vibrating music, blinding lights, his touch, and smell; it's overwhelming in the best way. I feel like I'm having an out-of-body experience. This is euphoria at its finest, and I've never felt freer and more reckless. My pleasure builds.

"Oh god," I moan.

He grabs my jaw, makes me look up at him, and says with a ruthless, raspy voice, "That's it, baby. But never say his name with me inside you ever again. It's Nico."

Of course, he has a sexy-as-fuck name. He moves his hand down to my throat with some added pressure. The act alone brings me to the edge of my orgasm. He watches me with such hunger, such feral need. No one has ever looked at me with pure starvation like that. I flutter my eyes shut and savor the euphoria of this moment.

I almost scream his name from the pleasure he's building in me. "Fuck, Nic—"

He interrupts me mid-moan and takes my mouth into his. The kiss is desperate, passionate, and sensual all at once. Like we were both dying for a taste. His tongue meets my mouth, demanding that I open. I give him access but shove my tongue in his mouth before he gets the chance to, taking the dominance from him. I bite his bottom lip and draw a hint of blood. His hand on my throat tightens, but I can still breathe plenty. Although that's debatable based on my panting. I lose control as my fingernails dig into the back of his neck, likely leaving marks. I grind on his fingers at a much faster pace, needing the release. Craving it. Desperate for it. He breaks the kiss, and the look on his face is pure lust.

His voice is strained when he demands, "Cum for me, baby."

I have never had an orgasm before, so this whole thing is new to me. I don't finish immediately at his words, wanting to rebel against his demands. Based on his hand tightening around my neck, I can tell he doesn't take disobeying lightly. His voice when he speaks again is deadly.

"Now," he orders.

I don't care about the people around me or what foul play comes out of my mouth. I don't even know what happens over the next few seconds as I lose control. At this moment, all I think about is him as I have my first-ever mind-blowing orgasm.

I moan breathlessly, "Oh, my fucking. Yes, Nico. Don't stop."

Once the pleasure has slightly calmed, I open my eyes and look back at him. He slowly takes his fingers out of me, raises them to my mouth, and taps my arousal against my lips.

"Lick them clean," he demands.

With a slow stroke of my tongue, I slide it up his fingers, then suck them whole, tasting my salty and sweet arousal. He watches my red lips close around them and groans.

He praises me with words. "Good girl."

I come back down from the high of my orgasm, and the reality of it all hits me like a boulder. I came here for money, not an orgasm. Even though it was so addicting, I wanted another.

I turn around so that my front is to his. He's still hard, but I can't let that distract me. I dance with him a little more, put my hands on his hips, and then slowly grab his wallet from his back pocket. He's too distracted by my tits to notice. I wore a very revealing dress for this reason, and it's doing what I hoped. I see Rosie from the corner of my eye and signal her over from behind Nico, but I don't break his eye contact, so he doesn't turn to look. She quietly comes up behind, I hand it to her, and then she scurries away quickly. The song ends.

"How about I take you somewhere else?" He asks.

As enticing as the offer is, I refuse and remove my body from the front of his. "Um, sorry, but I have to go. Nice meeting you Nico. Thanks for the orgasm."

I giggle and quickly make my way through the crowd. It's so full of people that I can hide myself well because I have a feeling he doesn't take no for an answer. My friends and I make it out the door and run to her car, laughing and almost falling over in our heels. I jump in and look behind to see Nico running out.

I scream at Gia, "GO!"

I can hear and smell the tires burning rubber by how hard she pushes on the gas. We're laughing so hard I think we could pee ourselves. Rosie hands me his wallet, and I look at its contents. His license reads *Nicolai Leone*, thirty-three years old. He has four credit cards, perfect. There's a wad of cash inside, with multiple one-hundred-dollar bills. Bingo baby.

I lean forward and fan the hundreds in front of them. "Ladies, consider mission accomplished."

We all squeal in joy and jam out to "Gold Digger" by Kanye West on our way home. I fooled Nico, and I fooled him well.

CHAPTER 4

Nicolai

What the fuck. I stand still in shock after getting turned down by her. I didn't even realize she walked away until I blinked.

"Fuck," I curse to myself.

I scramble through the crowd, trying to find her, which isn't easy when there are many other blondes in here and tall men powering over them. I catch a glimpse of her red lips and run to the door to where she's headed. By the time I make it outside, she's already in a white Mercedes speeding away.

You've got to be kidding me. "FUCK!"

I didn't even get her name; what was I thinking?

I've never felt that way with any woman before, so possessive and ravenous. I craved a taste of her like a man starved for days, on the brink of death. The smell of her arousal mixed with her vanilla, honey scent had me suffering slowly. And when she sucked my fingers clean with those plump lips, I thought I was going to cum in my pants. There's no way I could ever get enough of her. The whimpers and moans she made, how tight she was, the look on her face of absolute pleasure. I want it all and more.

I try to calm down and walk back into the club. I decide some gambling will cool off some steam. I walk up to the VIP lounge.

I signal at the dealer, "Deal me in."

I go to grab my wallet to throw a hundred in the pile and realize it's not there. That's weird; I'm pretty sure I put it there. I head down to my office and search every area where it could be. It's nowhere to be found, and I don't misplace my things. Wait a second. Did she? No. I wouldn't be that stupid.

Yet here I am. With no wallet and a woman with somewhere to be. She fucking stole from me. I'm the last person she should have chosen out of all the people she could have stolen from. I'm raging and I have not gotten this angry in a long time. I put my hands on my desk, lean over, and bow my head between my shoulders. I try to take some deep breaths, but they are not helping. I need to vent. I grab my keys and walk to the club basement. Only I have access to this room because I don't allow anyone to see me express any emotion of any kind. Even when I'm killing someone, I don't show anger or resentment. That's why I am so good at gambling; you can't have a poker face if your expression always remains the same.

The basement floor is concrete and stained with blood. A few punching bags hang around the room, and mirrors cover the walls. There's a wooden chair in the corner and a duffel bag filled with some fun playthings for my captives—well, fun for me, not fun for them.

I unbutton my shirt, pull it off, put on my Everlast boxing gloves, and start punching the bag. I hear faint vibrating music from upstairs, my punches, and ragged breathing. The punching still isn't enough to satisfy my anger though. I take off my boxing gloves and start throwing my hands.

After an hour of anger management, my hands are split open and dripping blood. My rage is much more in check now. No pain, no gain, right?

I decide enough is enough, clean up, bandage my hands, change, and go upstairs. Considering how late it is, the club is a lot less packed, but my men always stay for a while. I see Rocco sitting at the bar drinking. I take a seat next to him and signal for a whisky. Rocco looks over at me, but I don't have the patience to look back or deal with him. I can see his smirk out of the corner of my eye.

"Long night?" He questions arrogantly.

"You have no idea," I say.

He goes on even though you can tell I don't want to be bothered right now. "If I had a girl like that in my arms tonight, I'd be ecstatic."

He's walking on thin ice, even mentioning her. So what he said next is walking on the edge of death by my hands.

"Tell me, how did she feel?"

All I see is red. If this fucker weren't an important business deal, he'd be dead by now. I slowly look right into his eyes so he knows I mean it. My voice is cruel when it comes out of my mouth, but I don't care, business partner or not.

"Ever mention her again, you can consider this deal over and my gun in your mouth choking you to death," I say with zero hesitation or bluff.

I know he needs this deal as much as I do. He may have connections, but that doesn't bring in money, which he needs. He puts his hands up defensively, claiming he was joking. I didn't find it funny.

I down my whisky, enjoying the sting it leaves in its trace. I don't drink much or get drunk because I don't like to be disoriented when I gamble. Luckily, there was a safe in my office full of cash, so she didn't rob me completely for the night.

I walk upstairs and find the VIP room quite full. When it gets this late at night, the club is closed but only to the public. Men in the mafia have access and know the secret way in. This is when the real money-making happens. I walk over to the table, and one of the men gets up. Since I own the club, I always get a seat. I throw a hundred on the table, and they deal me in.

The secret to winning is not cheating like most amateurs try to

do. If you get caught cheating in my club, then you get killed.

Everyone is aware of this rule. The secret is knowing what the

fuck you're doing. I've been playing poker since I was born. My

parents taught me at a young age, so it's all I've ever known.

I look down at my hand and am quite satisfied with it.

One queen away from a royal flush, the best hand in the game,

and a guaranteed win. After two turns I got the card I needed.

The man across from me looks smug, clearly thinking he will

win. So, I place two more-hundred-dollar bills in the pile. A few

people back out, so all that's left is us two. He lays his hand

down, full house. I'm not going to lie; it's a good play but not

good enough. I place mine down and see him turn pale. He

leaves the room, pissed off and dissatisfied with himself. I play a

few more rounds and win the next two. Then, I purposely lose the third game. If I were to win every game tonight, the men would get pissed off. I can handle one or two men but not a dozen. Eventually, I call it a night, close the club, and go home.

I pull up to my modern, two-story, blacked-out home. It sits on a hill with no neighbors. I like my privacy, so I just bought all the surrounding land near me. Bulletproof windows cover most of the outside; I prefer natural lighting over lights. A garage sits in the back full of dozens of cars. You can never have too many, right?

I'm exhausted by the time I walk through the door. My house is way too big for just me, but I wasn't going to buy a fucking hut when I was house hunting. It's very well-designed and classy but bland. The walls downstairs are all black, with white marble countertops in the kitchen and grey furniture in the living room. I have more rooms in this house than I know what to do with, so a lot of them sit empty. The master bedroom upstairs has white walls and a king-size black bed. As comfy as it is, I can't sleep even if I wanted to. So I go to my garage, grab what I need, and get to work.

Hours go by, and I'm now sweating and even more exhausted than I was, but it was worth it. I take a step back to take in what I've done. I smile in satisfaction. My bedroom no longer has white walls; they're now the shade of cherry red, *just like her lips.*

I hop in the shower to get the paint off my body. The paint turns the water red as it drains, making me think of her. I haven't gotten her out of my head all night. The way her lips parted before I even touched her. Her sweet, addicting voice. How well she took my fingers in her pussy and mouth. My name on her lips. I don't typically like to lose control, but she makes me completely deranged. The mental image of her red lips around my cock has my cum plastering the shower tiles.

I leave the shower, dissatisfied with the fact she's not here.

She will not get away unpunished for fooling me. I will find her and be her own personal hell.

CHAPTER 5

Angelina

Even though I don't want to leave them, my friends pull up to the block near my house. Gia parks the car and shuts off the lights but stops me before I grab the door handle to leave.

"Are you sure you'll be alright?" Gia asks.

Rosie chimes in next, "We can go in with you. We know what your father is like, and this whole thing scares me for you."

"No, I'll be fine, I promise. I can handle him. I love you both for worrying, though." I reassure them of my safety and squeeze both their hands to comfort them.

I should be scared right now, and I am, but not as much as I know they are. They know about everything my father has done, but until I was legally an adult, none of us could do anything to get me out of his grasp. I'm nervous about getting caught. I don't know what my father would do, but I know it wouldn't be pretty.

I put on a brave face, left the car, and walked toward my house. I sneaked up to my window so no light sensors went off and climbed the vine. This wasn't easy in heels, so try adding alcohol to the equation.

"Mother fucker," I curse under my breath.

My heel catches on one of the twigs. I shake my foot around and lose patience with the damn thing. I shimmy my foot out of it and leave the heel. After all, I can just buy new ones with my four new credit cards. I slowly lift the windowsill, praying no one's noticed my arrival. As soon as I step inside my room and see that it's empty and my parents are still asleep, I accept that this was a successful mission, and do a little happy dance. My fists pound through the air, and I jump a few times but stop suddenly, remembering not to wake anyone.

I grab the bags I packed earlier and brace myself for what's to come. While my plan may have been successful, the leaving will not go smoothly. My father has kept me here like a caged animal that he never intends to let free. I can't go out, I'm not supposed to have friends, I was homeschooled by a hired tutor, and I am not allowed to have any electronics, but he doesn't need to know that I do. Should I go on? I'm done living under a rock. I have no idea why I can't just be a normal person. It's understandable why I am dreading telling him I am leaving out of fear, but at the same time, I cannot wait a second longer to live for me and not for my father.

I would avoid the confrontation by leaving the front door open— which would alert the security guards and my father, of course—but I'm done being scared, plus I need my car. My father has more than a dozen cars, so he gave me one after I begged repeatedly, but surprise, I could never take it anywhere. I take a deep breath, square my shoulders, and prepare for what's to come.

I turn the doorknob and immediately gasp, taken aback by my father standing in front of me like he was waiting there the whole time.

My father had brown hair when he was young, but it's turned grey in spots over the years. He uses too much hair gel every day to try to perfect his hair, and he wears so much cologne that I have to hold my breath. He has a tan skin tone that doesn't hide the wrinkles all over his face and body. He's a big guy, not only because of his muscles but because of what he was born with as well. Tall and big-boned, but not fat. I don't think I've ever seen him smile; he's either angry or expressionless around me and my mother, and never anything else. Right now, his face is very angry, and his arms are crossed over his chest, which isn't a good sign.

As I look around, I realize the security guard is nowhere to be found; the same was true of my mother. My father's arms are crossed, and he looks down at my bags. Then over my outfit, with disapproval written all over his face. Suddenly I'm uncomfortable and slightly frightened, but not backing down.

"Going somewhere?" my father asks with a clipped edge to his tone.

Typically, I weaken under my father's stare, keep my head down, and avoid eye contact, but it's time for a change. I refuse to leave as the sad, weak girl my father thinks he raised. Tonight, I leave as a strong, independent woman who raised herself.

I lift my chin and meet his eyes when I say, "I'm leaving."

He laughs, but I don't find this moment comical.

"With what money?" he asks.

"I can support myself," I shoot back. He doesn't need to know where I got my money; all that matters is that I have it.

He scoffs and shakes his head. "Yeah, okay, Angelina, very funny. Unpack your bags. You're not going anywhere."

Excuse me? I've never refused my father's orders, but there's a first for everything.

I stand my ground with a firm, "No."

I try to push past him with my bags, but he grabs my arm. I look down and wince.

"You will let me go," I say. I don't show him weakness or whine how much his grip hurts me. In all seriousness, though, I will have bruises tomorrow.

His voice is furious when he speaks in a tone louder than before. "I gave you everything. Food, clothes, a roof, and even luxuries. This is how you treat your father!"

He's shouting at this point, and maybe the angriest I've ever seen him, but I am so done at this point. I am exhausted; he has pulled my strings far too thin to back down.

I yank my arm out of his grip and confidently say something I've always wanted to say, "You're no father to me."

He backhands me as the words leave my mouth. I can't even lift my head, taken aback by what he just did. I taste copper on my tongue and unbearable pain on my face. I knew he wouldn't take this well, but I didn't think he would ever lay a hand on me. He's always hit my mother but never me. One thing is for sure, he will never do that to me again.

I lift my head and feel the blood dripping from my mouth, but I don't wipe it off. I meet his stare head-on and spit the blood in his face. He winces, not expecting me to do that. I know his blood is boiling at this point, so I pass him while I have the chance. I hurry down the stairs, grab the keys to my red

Audi R8, and leave. I speed out of the driveway, furious, hurt, and proud of myself. I'm overwhelmed with emotions, but I don't cry. He doesn't deserve my tears.

I drive for miles until I find a hotel to my liking. I find one in town, covered in polished gold and white. The lights make it pop compared to every other building around. I pull up to the front doors and open my door to an older gentleman in a tuxedo. I hand him my keys to park my car, and two other gentlemen grab my bags from my trunk. I check in at the front desk and pay for the night, which ends up emptying all the cash in Nico's wallet. Luckily, he has plenty of credit cards, so I'm not broke just yet.

I take the elevator to my room, and my jaw is on the floor when I walk through my door. There's a white king-size bed in the middle, with not a single wrinkle on it. A hanging chandelier above, and multiple windows with a stunning view of the town and lights below. A large TV hangs on the wall across from the bed. I look up, and I'm completely speechless. Every bit of the ceiling is a mirror, and I love it. I move toward the bathroom, and it's just as good as I expected. A stand-up shower with glass doors and a white marble interior. Stocked with high-quality shampoo, conditioner, and body wash. A towel warmer sits to the side, and washcloths, towels, and even a robe are on the rack. This hotel room is a dream, and I have Nico to thank.

CHAPTER 6

Nicolai

I'm convinced that I dreamt of last night. I've looked and asked around everywhere for this mystery woman; it's like she doesn't exist. It would help a whole fucking lot if I knew her name. I'm pissed off and losing my sanity all over one girl. She's distracting every part of me, my work, my poker game, hell I haven't even been to the club once today because I'm too busy fucking around for this woman who may or may not exist. But she did, and my wallet disappeared with her.

Hours go by, and I still have gotten nowhere. Every corner is a dead end. There are too many blondes in this town, and I have nothing else besides her physical description to go off. I've asked people who look her age and local businesses, and I've even resorted to researching online. Typically, I can find people easily. I have connections, and everybody knows everybody. But no one knows her. Either she doesn't want to be found, or someone's hiding her.

I go to the club and take my mind off things before I lose my temper. I play a few games of poker and lose one—but this time not on purpose. Which pisses me off. I don't lose, but I can't show my anger to the other men. I excuse myself to make a phone call, and Enzo picks up after the first ring.

"Bring him in," I say over the phone.

A half-hour later I go to the only place that helps release the tension in my shoulders.

Punch after punch, but this time not a bag, but rather a scum fuck of a man. He wails in pain, and I savor every sound. I only do the beating when I'm pissed off, and they deserve it, and he sure fucking does.

He cries and pleads, "Please let me go. I'll give you whatever you want. Money, my car, anything!"

He says the last word breathlessly, and it looks as if he may pass out at any moment. That won't do; he needs to be awake for all of it. That is precisely why I grab his face, spit in it, and break his nose with a loud crack.

I laugh and say to him, "I have everything, don't you see? Your money, car, even that scared look in your eyes won't get you out of this one."

I grab the baseball bat leaning against the wall, raise it above my head, and bring it down on his kneecap. I smile at the gory sight of his bone now poking out of his skin. He screams and cries, which is quite frankly annoying to talk over, so I pour gasoline down his throat to shut him up. The sound of his gargles and pungent smell fills the basement.

The floor is coated in his blood, piss, teeth, and gasoline. Honestly, I don't know how he's still alive.

I lean down, put my hands on the arms of his chair, and look into his fucking soul. As much as I'd love to kill him already, I have questions, and he has answers.

I lean down to the arms of the chair and look dead into his eyes when I ask, "Does the name Leone ring a bell?"

I catch a hint of hesitation, barely any, and I'm sure anyone but me wouldn't have noticed it. Sucks for him.

"No man, I have no idea who that is."

Liars piss me off, if only he knew that. I punch him in his face again, covering the concrete floor in even more bloodshed.

I circle his chair, come behind him, and squeeze his shoulders with enough grip to break them. "That's weird because I recall you working security the night of their deaths. Want to explain to me where the footage from that night went? Hm?"

His face pales, and he denies all of it. Fucking liar. I shoot him, but not in the face. No, the scum doesn't deserve a fast death. I shoot him in the leg, the one without the bone poking out, and leave him to bleed out painfully.

I motion to my employees. "Clean up this mess. If I find out you showed any mercy to him, you'll suffer the same fate or worse."

After they nod their head, I slam the door shut on my way out.

I'm so fucking sick of dead ends.

I did everything I could to get information out of him about my parents' death. He wouldn't let up and wasn't going to. He had a haunted look in his eyes. He knows who killed them but would rather go to the grave than be a rat.

CHAPTER 7

Angelina

I have never felt so free but so lost at the same time. My entire life was dictated by my father; I don't know who I am without someone controlling everything I do and am. I won't sit around any longer, or this will become a pity party for one. I put my makeup on heavy enough to hide the bruises forming. I throw on jeans and a tee and meet my friends for dinner at a pasta restaurant near the hotel. As soon as they see me, they're beaming and look relieved to see I'm alive.

"Ahh, how does it feel to be a free woman!" Rosie screams.

"Oh my gosh, Angelina we are so going out tonight to celebrate," Gia chimes in while jumping up and down and clapping her hands.

"Well, duh!" I say while going in for a hug with them both.

Gia looks at Rosie and says, "Omg, what are we going to do with her now? I have been waiting for this for so long! We could take her to the strip club, or skydiving, or—"

I put my hands on her shoulders and cut her off before she goes too far or passes out from not breathing in between her words.

"Gia, I love you but one step at a time," I say.

We sit down at the table. We've never really had a chance to catch up without something rushing me home so I could talk and listen to them for hours.

"Okay, spill. How's private school been?" I ask.

Both of them have been going to private school since they were kids. I used to be jealous that they could socialize with others in a school setting until they told me about the children there. They're all spoiled assholes. Hearing about it made me grateful that my parents had me tutored and graduated with a GED at home.

Gia groans and says with misery, "Ugh. It's been hell. Thank God we only have one more month, or I swear I'd lose my shit with those preppy bitches."

For Gia to call someone a bitch and speak unkindly truly means they are what she says they are. She doesn't speak that way about anyone unless they deserve it.

Rosie adds, "No kidding. Gia had to hold me back from slapping Alexandra Bianchi after she was talking shit about her and spitting rumored lies."

Rosie and Gia have always had drama with Alex Bianchi. I don't know her myself since my father hid me from the world, but I know enough about her to know she is a total bitch.

"Damn, I would've let you slap her. Someone needs to knock some sense into her," I say.

"See! Thank you. It's probably for the best that she stopped me, though. My parents would have lost it if I tampered our reputation with violence," Rosie says.

Gia interrupts before I ask anything more about their social lives. "Okay, okay. Enough about school. You haven't told us how your dad handled last night."

I was trying to avoid the subject and distract them with other topics, but that didn't last long. The last thing I want is to see their faces when I tell them he hit me and see weakness. I refuse to look weak in front of anyone any longer.

I lie, "Better than I thought. He was upset, as I expected, but he let me go and kept his emotions intact. I told you it'd be fine."

Rosie watches me carefully as if she can see right through my lie but doesn't call me on it. She stays quiet.

Gia, on the other hand, always breaks the silence. "It's about damn time he let you do something for yourself. Maybe he's finally trying to correct his wrongs and make you happy."

Yeah right.

"One can hope," I say.

We talk some more, but not about my father. We dropped the subject after the question because they knew I didn't like talking about him. Hours fly by when we catch up with one another. After dinner, Gia and Rosie suggest a night out, and I couldn't agree more. I can do whatever I want now, and if you thought my nights as a gold digger were over, you're far from wrong. We get up to leave, but then a thought dawns on me.

There's a hint of panic in my voice. "Wait. I have nothing to wear."

It was impossible to buy the clothes I liked at my father's. I had no money, and he had to approve all of it. I wasn't allowed skirts, short dresses, tight jeans, or short shorts. The only reason I had a black dress the other night was all thanks to Rosie.

"This calls for a shopping emergency!" Gia squeals happily.

Rosie agrees, "I'm down."

I smile because I'd love nothing more than to shop with my best friends with my new credit cards.

There's an outdoor mall not far from the hotel, so Gia drives us there in hopes of finding me an outfit for tonight. We've walked for half an hour and gone inside a few stores but haven't found anything yet. We pass a lingerie store and Gia stops in her tracks.

Gia turns me and Rosie around. "Not so fast. We are so going in."

I roll my eyes but don't refuse. I could always use a new matching set.

I find a black bra and thong and try them on. The bralette is triangular-shaped, with black lace, but not dark enough to cover my nipples. It's very see-through despite the color, but I like it. The panties are less of a thong and more of a G-string. The straps are thin, and the panties are so small they barely cover anything, but I don't mind that. I buy the set, disregarding the price. Eighty-five euros later, I walk out with a bag of what I'll be wearing tonight underneath my outfit, that is if I find one.

We go to a few more boutiques in search of a dress, but nothing speaks to me. I almost give up until we round the corner, and a dress in the window display catches my eye. I stop walking and put my hand on the girls' shoulders to signal them to look, too. We go inside and I immediately get a fitting room. I put it on, and it fits snugly, but just the way I like it. I look in the mirror and take it in. It's red and sleeveless, with a short pencil skirt and open cleavage through a V-neck down to the skirt. It stops above my knees and hugs my ass. The top half is so tight that it pushes my tits together. I won't need my new bra with this dress, but at least I can still wear my new panties. It's beyond perfect. I step outside to show the girls, but they're speechless. I've never seen them speechless before; then again, they hardly ever see me dressed up like this.

"That dress was made for you," Rosie says.

"Stop it right now. I'm going to cry." Gia wipes her eyes.

"Ugh, I love you guys so much, and this dress," I add in.

Of course, I bought the dress but ran out of cash from my expensive hotel. I had to pay with a credit card for my lingerie and dress and will have to use it for the rest of the night. Gia drives back to the hotel where we fix our makeup, change into club attire, and do our hair. I straighten mine so it can flow smoothly down the dress and around my tits. I'm about to walk out the door with them when my phone vibrates in my purse. I pull it out and read the text.

Father: Come home, and we can talk this out.

Gia notices my pause.

"You, okay?"

I don't reply to his text. I turn my Do Not Disturb on and stuff my phone into my purse.

"Yeah, just stupid spam. Let's go." I say as I plaster on a smile.

I will never go back to my father, at least not permanently. Maybe someday I'll visit, but not for him, for my mom. I'm on my own now financially, and until I find a job, gold-digging will have to do. Tonight, I'll find a man interested

and steal his wallet, just like I did to Nico.

CHAPTER 8

Nicolai

My phone dings in my pocket, and I take it out to see the eighty-five euro charge at a lingerie store. I grin. *I bought it, so I will find her and make her show me.* Half an hour later, another charge of $170 at a boutique. I was wondering when she'd start spending. Although I can prevent more spending by calling my bank for fraud, I don't. She intrigues me too much, and I find satisfaction in knowing that she's spending my money. The boutique is not far from here, which reassures me that she didn't run off with my wallet to some other state, *thank God*. But I would've followed her anywhere.

An hour goes by that I spend running the club. Doing rounds, approving paperwork, small talk with my employees, and much more meticulous bullshit to keep this place in check.

My phone dings in my pocket, and I pull it out to reveal another charge to my card.

Twenty-four euros at Serata di Sogno Club.

Fuck no. That's where I draw the line. She can spend my money on anything, gas, clothes, food, whatever she wants but that. No way in hell is she spending it in a club that's not mine and dancing on another man. I grab my keys to my black Lamborghini and leave, not giving a damn about work anymore. I speed down the road, passing other cars along the way. What was a thirty-minute drive turns into ten. By the time I pull in, I am way more pissed than I was when I left. I slam my car door shut, push past the line of people, and make my way inside.

Serata di Sogno is a club I try to avoid. It's dingy for my taste. It's technically a club for the rich, but the security is so lazy that you can fake it or sneak in. I guarantee half of the people in this club are poor people pretending to have money or rich pricks with bad intentions. It's a nice club on the inside and out, but compared to my club, it looks like shit.

It's a smaller building than mine and fills up quickly. The club is packed with people, which makes me even angrier. It'll be nearly impossible to spot her. As I'm walking around, a few women approach me, asking for a drink. I tell them I'm not interested and nicely move them out of my way. This is precisely why I made my club members-only exclusive. I can't stand the crowd in here. I make it up to the bar in the middle, a blue-lit-up circular table with drinks and bartenders in the middle. I order a Jack to ease some of my tension.

I take a sip, and right as I raise my glass to my lips I stop and see her across the bar. The first thing I notice is her red lips; they are what sets her apart from everyone else. Then I notice what she's wearing. A tight red dress that hugs her in all the right places and exposes plenty. It makes my dick strain painfully against my pants. Her hair is straightened this time, and all I can think about is how I can wrap it around my fist three times. She is far down the table and won't see me through the chaos of people ordering drinks in front of me. She's sipping on a drink with her friends, the same ones from the other night.

A guy walks up to her from behind, looks her up and down, and then puts his fucking hand on her lower back. I almost shatter the glass in my hand by how hard I am gripping it. He asks to buy her another drink, and she nods. Her friends part ways, so it's just him and her left. My blood boils, but I don't intervene just yet. I watch her every move. I slowly make my way around, getting a little closer, hiding behind others, and careful to not let her spot me. Unlike how she did with me, she avoids eye contact with this guy. She smiles a few times, but I can tell they're fake. She isn't attracted to this guy, so why is she flirting with him?

He motions at the bartender for a cranberry vodka. He pays and moves the drink forward; at that moment, she looks away. Like she's looking for her friends. In the millisecond that she's distracted, he reaches into his pocket, pours a dusty substance into the drink, and stirs. While he does that, I think of all the ways he will die painfully. I make a quick phone call to an employee and tell him the club I'm at, as well as his description.

I make my demands clear. "Make it painful and slow. He deserves to suffer. Oh, and I want his hand chopped off."

No one touches my girl and lives to see the next day. I end the call quickly before he can hand her the drink. I walk up to them, ignoring her momentarily which is killing me, and grab him by the collar.

I push him toward me and look into his eyes. My voice is deadly when I whisper to him. "Next time you want to slip something in someone's drink, think twice. That's my girl, and I will kill you with my bare hands."

Then I deck him in the face to give him a small taste of the beating he will receive tonight.

CHAPTER 9

Angelina

The good news is that I found a guy who looks wealthy enough to be worth my time. The bad news is that I am not attracted to him and am disinterested in this boring conversation. I let him buy me a drink, leading him on until I can steal his wallet. I look for my friends but have no luck spotting them. The crowd is so big it's nearly impossible. Every time I look into his eyes I want to vomit. Every part of him gives me the ick, from his unkempt, greasy brown hair and scrawny build to his taste in alcohol, which is a martini. What kind of a guy drinks a martini? I am so turned off by him that it's not even funny. My mouth hurts from fake smiling so much. I thank him for my drink and am about to take a sip but stop when something coming up to us catches my eye. Is that? Oh shit.

I look at him and ask with a hint of panic in my voice.

"Nico, what are you doing here?"

"Not now, baby," he says back without looking at me.

He stares down the guy next to me with pure anger in his eyes. The guy sinks in his seat, clearly threatened by his size. Nico grabs him by his striped collar shirt, whispers something in his ear, and then punches him in the face. The guy tries to contain the blood from gushing out of his nose and quickly scurries away with a scared expression written on his face. Suddenly, I realize the situation I'm in. I stole from this man, and he knows it too.

I avoid his eyes. "Um, Nico, it's great seeing you and all, but my friends just texted, and they need me."

I try to get up and leave, but he traps me as I spin my chair around. His arms lean on the table, on both sides of me, with no way to get out. He's so close I can feel his breath on my lips. I look down at them, suddenly craving a taste. I look up into his eyes and see that he's looking at my lips just like I was his. He moves his eyes back up to mine.

"Not happening. You're with me for the night," he says.

As threatening as this man is, I feel oddly safe with him. I give up my fight, knowing that he won't hurt me and that I want his company. Maybe he doesn't even know I stole from him? I mean, he's filthy rich. I'm sure it didn't even phase him. He dumps out my drink. I give him a look of What the fuck did you just do that for.

He says, "He drugged that, but don't worry, he will pay for it."

My mouth opens, and no words come out of it. Oh my god, imagine if I drank that. I could've been raped, for god's sake. I need to be less careless with my actions; I'm just not used to being out like this.

He motions at the bartender and orders me a new one. I watch my drink the whole time, but I'm certain Nico wouldn't drug me; I have a feeling he's not the type to do that. I didn't realize until now that my mouth was still slightly gaped open out of pure shock that I was almost drugged.

He leans in close to me and says, "Close that pretty red mouth of yours, or I'll give you a reason to open wider."

His dirty words and serious tone make me clench my thighs together. I change the subject, desperate for a distraction.

"So…" My voice comes out high-pitched, and I have to cough to fix my nerves when I speak. "What are you doing at a club like this when you have one much better back in Milan?"

He smirks as if he knows how he affects me. "I was in town for business and wanted a drink nearby."

After a few minutes, he motions for the bartender, noticing my drink getting low. I didn't pay attention before, but he's still working on his first one. I wonder what a guy like Nico drinks. Letting the alcohol in my system do my thinking, I impulsively grab his glass, bring my lips to the rim, and sip it. Whisky, I should have guessed. It made me flinch at first, but I liked it. It's rich and smooth, with a hint of burn.

I stop the bartender before he starts my typical drink of choice. "I'll take what he's having."

When I hand Nico his glass back, I realize my lips left a red imprint on the glass. He grabs it from my hand, and his fingers touch mine. I suck in a breath, shocked by the heat of his touch. He brings the glass to his lips without breaking eye contact and drinks right where my lips touched. He licks his lips where there's a hint of red, and I track every movement of his tongue. Is it hot in here? I down my new whiskey in one gulp and hold back the pain it brings down my throat. He leans in and puts his hand on my exposed thigh.

"That's my girl," he says with his deep voice. I love it when he calls me that.

I feel my cheeks turn red from blushing.

Shortly after, I have a good buzz. I feel careless and free and damn good. I suggest a game, and I can tell he's intrigued.

"Truth or dare?" I ask.

He seems like a daring type of guy, but he surprises me with the truth.

I think hard and come up with a question I knew he had lied about earlier. "Why were you really in this club tonight?"

He hesitates, then says, "I was looking for you."

While I'm zoned in on what he just admitted, he asks me for a truth or dare, and I say the truth.

"What's your name?" he asks with a curious glint in his stare.

Now, that I did not expect. I shouldn't tell him, considering I stole from him, and he could report me to authorities. That's the exact reason I haven't told him. But if he knew I stole from him, would he be sitting with me right now?

"Angelina," I admit.

He shakes his head and looks into my soul.

"Bellissima…" runs smoothly off his tongue.

"Truth or dare," I ask again.

He grins but not in the sweet manner he has been; no, this grin is full of evil.

"I'm warning you, don't dare me to do things because I will do them."

I lean down and in towards him, purposely giving him a full view of my cleavage. He can't tear his eyes away from my chest. I can see the fire in his eyes and how much he wants me. I get so close to him that I put my lips against his ear.

I whisper, "I dare you to take me on a drive."

I really, really should not leave with a stranger, let alone a stranger I stole from, but the alcohol is doing the talking tonight. I text my friends and tell them I'm leaving, and I'll be safe. Then I walk out the door hand in hand with a man that I know is dangerous, but our game isn't over just yet.

CHAPTER 10

Nicolai

I thought I was losing it before; now, look at me. I'm a fucking mess. I'm still fuming because of that prick. What if I wasn't there? My mind is racing with the what-ifs and with her. She looks incredible tonight, and earlier, when she teased my eyes with her tits, I almost took her over my shoulder out of here. Luckily, she suggested we leave so I didn't have to get turned down again, asking to go elsewhere.

We make it to my car, and she whistles. "Nice ride."

"Get in."

I hop in the driver's seat, and then she's next in the passenger seat. I watch as she sits down, her dress moving further up as she gets comfortable, exposing her smooth, tan legs. I look away and try to control my hard-on from ripping my pants or her noticing. I lock the car doors and see her tense from the corner of my eye. Good. I'm tired of her having so much control over me; it's time I make her feel how she makes me feel, stupidly helpless.

I break the silence. "I love that dress. It had to cost a fortune. $170, was it?"

I can see her freaking out internally, thinking of all the ways to get out of this situation.

"I'm so sorry. I can pay you back every penny. I didn't think you'd notice…"

I bring my thumb to her lips to quiet her, trace it across the bottom, and smear her red lipstick. I've been dying to do that, along with many other things.

"Oh, baby, I'm not upset; there's no need to apologize," I say.

She has a confused look on her face, and I continue.

"I take that back. I'm upset you fooled me so easily, but I'm also impressed. Only you could get away with stealing from me."

She's shivering under my touch, and I can see her hard nipples through her dress. Oh, she's helpless, alright, but I never want her to feel unsafe with me, so I ease up.

I lean back into my seat. "Keep the cards and money. I don't care how much money you take or if you use me for it. But mark my words, you're going to earn it."

Her breath hitches, and she crosses her legs. I grin, loving how I'm making her squirm.

I leave the parking lot and head toward the hotel she said she's staying at. I don't want to be done with her yet, so I continue her game.

"Truth or dare?"

"Dare," she says.

That's my girl.

Seeing her unraveling before me, all breathless, turned on, and wearing that has made my restraint snap. I'm trying to take it slow with her, but I can't. She wants me as much as I want her, and if I can't have her right here, right now, all hell will break loose.

I keep my eyes on the road as I say, "Get on your knees and lean over the console."

With zero hesitation, she listens. Seeing her bent over in my car almost made me pull over and take her this instance, but I decided against it. She deserves more than a quick car fuck. I can see the lust in her eyes and the pure need for more. I won't fuck her, but I'll at least give her a taste. I undo my belt with one hand still on the wheel, unzip my pants, and pull my raging hard-on out. She stares at it, looking intimidated and nervous. I take her jaw in my hand, forcing her to look into my eyes. That way, if she lies, I'll be able to tell.

"Have you never done this before?" I ask.

She shakes her head, and I am speechless, in awe of her. My innocent little angel.

"Fanculo mi. Che cosa mi stai facendo bambina?" I whisper under my breath.

She's never done this with any other man, which turns me on more than I'd like to admit.

"Suck," I demand, refusing to wait any longer.

She leans down, and as she does, her ass rises over the center console.

"Tell me, angel. Are you wearing the panties I bought you?" I ask as I trace one hand up her thigh and keep the other on the wheel.

She slowly licks her tongue along the bottom of my shaft to the top, placing a red kiss on top. She then moans a sweet "mmhmm" to answer my question. Seeing the red imprint of her lips on my cock has me groaning and holding onto my control for dear life. She swallows my size whole and sucks up and down at an ungodly rhythm sending me to the edge already. If this is heaven, I'll get on my hands and knees and pray to God for forgiveness to stay out of hell.

I tap below the hem of her dress, requesting permission, and she nods her head while continuously sucking me. I reach under, pull down a black, lacy thong, and take it off her body. I pocket them. *Those are mine now.*

"Buy new ones because you aren't getting those back," I tell her.

She takes me as far as she can, hitting the back of her throat. I take deep breaths and try my best to keep from exploding all over her face.

"Such a good girl," I praise while petting her hair.

The sight of her swallowing my cock, ass in the air, and tits falling out of her dress could bring any man to his knees. I hit a pothole on accident, and she gags. While I didn't do that on purpose, I savor the sound of her gagging from my size.

"Sorry, mio angelo, accident, I swear." I laugh under my breath.

As if she doesn't believe me, she lightly scrapes her teeth on my cock as she brings her head up. I fist her hair and tug on it so her ear is next to my lips.

"Do that again, and I'll punish you mercilessly for it. And I'll love every second of it." My voice is gravelly and labored when it comes out.

I can feel her grinning on my cock, loving the idea of punishment. I swear to God she will be the death of me. She's a goddess at blowing, for it being her first time, making me wonder what else she's good at. She squirms and lifts her dress giving me a view of her bare ass over my console. *Fuck me.*

She stops sucking momentarily, and I slap her ass for it. She leans back down and does something that makes me lose all control I was holding. She deepthroats me again and grabs a handful of my balls while sucking. I move her head up and down at the pace I need. Looking down at her, seeing her eyes water, throat bobbing, and red lipstick smeared all over my cock makes me explode in her mouth.

"Fuck. That's it. Be my good girl and swallow," I demand.

She swallows my release, but some slips out of her mouth as she eases up.

"Clean up your mess, mio angelo," I tell her.

She licks up the rest of me and swallows again as I pull into the hotel parking lot. As much as I want to return the favor and feel how wet she is under her dress, I can tell she's exhausted, so I walk her to her room. I'll be back for her anyway, eager to make her just as pleased as she made me.

I tuck her in and then head to her bathroom. I grab the makeup wipes after rifling through the cabinets looking for them. I come back out to her, barely awake. I sit on the bed beside her, brush wisps of her hair off her face, and wipe off her makeup. She's even more naturally beautiful than I could have imagined. She falls asleep peacefully while I gently remove it.

I move onto the other half of her face but stop wiping when something catches my attention. There's a faint purple bruise and finger marks on her left cheek where someone hit her.

I just got over the other fucking guy, and now I find out

someone hit her?

I'm not one to lose control of my anger, but since

meeting her, my temper has been restless, and it's on the brink

of uncontrollable. Just looking at the bruise makes my heart rate

accelerate, and the room suddenly feels too small. My thoughts

are racing at a dangerous rate. Who did this? Did this happen

before or after we met? Is it my fault? Is she okay?

I need to get out of here and punch something, or my

impulsive side will wake her up and demand answers. I grab her

phone and punch my number in. I'm not losing her again. She

has hundreds of texts, from her friends to her mother and father.

But I don't read them; it's not my business to. Yet, I can't help

myself when one catches my attention.

Father: I'm sorry for hitting you. I just hated the thought of losing you so much that my body took over my rational thoughts. Come home. Your mother misses you.

I don't care if this guy is her father or not. I will end him for hurting her. This guy is supposed to be her protector, not her fucking abuser. I plug her phone into the charger, lean down, and kiss her forehead.

"Sweet dreams, mio angelo," I whisper.

I leave and head to the club to release some anger before I kill someone for simply looking at me the wrong way.

CHAPTER 11

Angelina

I wake up to a raging headache and on the cliff of vomiting all over my bed. My dress is still on, but my makeup is off when I look in the mirror. Everything comes rushing back to me. The club, the game, the drive home, Nico putting me to bed. I slightly recall falling asleep to his hands on my face in smooth strokes, and the thought of him taking care of me makes my heart flutter a thousand beats too fast. Then I remember the undeniable bruise on my face, *shit*. There's no way he didn't see it.

I remember bits and pieces of the car ride home. His black Lamborghini with black leather seats, the pure lust in his eyes, the scent of whisky and arousal filling up the small space, him pocketing my new panties, and how big he was. It was all too much to handle, so why do I want it all over again?

I pull on a pair of leggings and a tee shirt, then brush my hair out, at least looking a little presentable for my friends. They texted me this morning, letting me know they're on their way over to meet up. I make my way to the elevator and press the lobby button. The movement of the elevator makes my stomach churn, but I hold back the vomit.

Once I see Gia and Rosie in the lobby, they speed-walk toward me, and their voices are way too loud for my preference. I signal toward the food before we spill the tea. We make a quick plate at the buffet and then sit down at a table away from others.

I groan. "I swear you guys are screaming, and I have the worst hangover ever."

Gia reality checks me. "Girl, you look like shit."

"Oh my god, what happened to your face?! Did that guy hurt you last night because I swear to g—" I interrupt Rosie before her thoughts spiral.

"No, he didn't hurt me. My—" I stop talking.

I literally cannot think of anything to excuse my face, and they won't stop staring at me for an answer. I set my fork down that's full of a delicious waffle, and syrup oozing from it. I probably would have thrown it up anyway.

"I didn't want to tell you guys because I don't want pity looks."

They look at me with worry and wait for me to go on.

I sigh. "My father did this the night I left. He didn't take it as well as I let on."

They kind of just stare for a beat, then two. Gia stands abruptly.

She puts her hands up. "Oh, hell to the no."

She tries to leave but I grab her hand and advise her to sit down.

Rosie shakes her head and says, "I fucking knew he didn't take it well. My gut was telling me, but I ignored it."

Even though they're pissed, I smile because they don't look at me with pity or weakness like I expected. They just look at me like they want to kill my father, and that's okay.

I try to calm them. "You have every right to be mad. I am, too. He's been blowing up my phone, but I haven't said a word to him. The last thing I want you to do is get involved. This is my fight to handle."

Rosie puts her hand over mine. "Well, you're not alone. Ever need someone to step in and throw some hands you know who to call," she says.

They back off the subject and let up. I'm so grateful for friends who are as understanding and caring as they are.

Gia crosses her arms. "So, are you going to tell us what happened last night with the mystery guy or make us sit here and suffer even longer?"

I smile at the thought of Nico. "It was my idea to leave the club with him. I let the alcohol get the best of me. Whisky gets me fucked up."

They make disgusted faces at the mention of whisky, making me laugh. They're more of the lemon drop shots and sex on the beach type of gals.

"He drove me home, and things got heated in the car. Let's just say he doesn't disappoint." I wink at them and they both gasp.

"Omg, Angelina, did you lose your V-card? We have to get a cake and celebrate. This is a crucial moment we've all been waiting for!" Gia says way too loudly in a public hotel cafeteria.

"No, virginity is still intact." I lean down, lower my voice, and add, "Just maybe not in the oral department."

They try to scream quietly, but it's not quiet in any way.

"Shh." I can't stop giggling at their giddiness. We're acting like a bunch of teenage girls, but I don't care.

"Look at little Angelina growing up. You're becoming one hell of a woman, and very quickly, might I add," Rosie says.

"So, like, on a scale of one to ten." Gia gestures with her hands his dick size.

"Maybe like eleven?" I put my hands up in question.

"Angelina Vittori!" They both say in unison.

"Okay, but in all seriousness, didn't you steal from this guy?" Rosie asks.

She is always the logical friend of the group, whereas Gia is still probably thinking about his dick size.

"Yeah, and he knows it. At first, I was terrified I got caught. My life flashed before my eyes. Then he said he wasn't mad. He said I can keep his cards and spend his money, just not on other clubs or men."

They just sit there in shock with their mouths wide open.

"Does he have any brothers?" Gia asks, not at all joking.

Rosie points her finger at me. "You just got yourself the hottest, youngest sugar daddy on the planet. Your gold digger days are over."

"Don't get me wrong, I'm glad, but Nico feels like more to me than just his money. Every time I'm around him, my entire body tingles, I forget to breathe, and he makes me feel like I'm on fire." My cheeks turn red talking about him.

"You've got it bad." Emphasis on the word bad by Gia.

Rosie nods her head in agreement.

My phone dings, taking my attention away from this conversation. I almost ignore it, thinking it's my father again, but my gut nudges me to look.

Nico: Morning, angel. How are you feeling?

My heart soars out of my chest seeing his name on the screen.

Angelina: Like someone just ran me over and then kicked me in the head five times. How'd you get my number?

Nico: I punched it in my phone right after you fell asleep. Problem?

Angelina: Always a problem with you.

Nico: Says the little pickpocketer. Watch it, or I'll punish you later for that attitude. Don't think I forgot about your teeth stunt last night. Your tallies are adding up quickly.

"Ahem."

Rosie's voice brings me out of my trance.

"Oh shit, sorry, I got distracted. What were you saying?"

I ask with a slight giggle.

They both look at me with their eyebrows tilted and arms

crossed.

"It's him, isn't it?" Rosie asks.

"Was it that obvious?" I ask with an apologetic tone.

"Girl, you're tomato red from head to toe," Gia says.

"Just be careful. We don't want to see you get hurt. I

mean, you barely know the guy." Rosie's realistic senses hit me

in the chest.

"I appreciate you looking out for me, but I can handle

my own," I tell her, even though she's right.

We talked and ate some breakfast for a few more minutes

and then said our goodbyes. The food cured my hangover so

much that I feel like it's starting to fade away.

My phone dings in my pocket as I wait for the elevator to go up to my room.

Nico: Make those four tallies now for ignoring me.

Angelina: You mean three?

Nico: Nope. Fourth is for stealing and fooling me. You didn't think I'd let you get away that easily, did you?

I decide to push him further because I'm having too much fun poking the bear.

Angelina: You know I have a life. I can't text you twenty-four-seven and you aren't my number one priority at the moment.

Nico: You're mine.

My face heats, and my heart flutters. He can be so sweet and ruthless at the same time.

CHAPTER 12

Nicolai

I call Angelina, already missing the sweet sound of her voice. It rings a few times before she finally answers.

"Clingy much?" She asks in her cute voice.

"Oh, this is nothing. I'm taking you out, so I'll pick you up in twenty. There's a great steak house that just opened nearby," I say back.

"Aw, Nico! How kind of you to ask! Hm, give me a minute while I think about it," she says.

"Angel," I say with little patience in my tone.

"Still thinking!" She shouts over the phone.

"Angelina," my voice is more stern this time.

I don't typically use her full name, but she's pushing my limits here, and she knows it.

"Okay, okay. That sounds lovely, but I'm having dinner with my parents. They've been begging to see me ever since I moved out, and I finally gave in," she says.

Either she has a soft spot for family, or she's making this up because as I recall, her father hit her. An incoming call interrupts our conversation, and I have no choice but to take it. If I had more time, I would get more information from her.

"Bummer. I have to go. Expect my call soon, mio angelo, and next time, I won't take no for an answer," I tell her as I say goodbye.

I end the call, upset that she may have just blown me off. She turns me down more often than anyone ever has, and I don't like it.

I answer the other call. My patience is slim, but I control my erratic breathing.

"What is it?" I ask.

"Hey, boss. Remember that guy from the other night that you told me to take care of?" My employee's voice speaks through the phone, annoying me for interrupting my conversation with her.

"What about him?"

"Well, I uh left him to bleed out on the floor, and when I went back in half an hour later expecting to find him dead, he was gone," he admits with fear in his voice.

Thank God for Rocco. Without his help with the cops, they'd be on my ass about this.

"You're fired," I say.

I end the call, furious with my employee's lack of control. I go downstairs and blow off some steam in the basement for a few hours to control my temper. Once I feel like I can finally breathe normally, I return to my office to make a call.

The multiple calls to my partner go to voicemail. He always answers, so I start to get worried. I grab my keys and head out the door towards his place. Enzo keeps his business and personal life very separate, so I have never been to his house. I've never had to because I've never had trouble getting ahold of him until now.

I pull into his driveway and put my car in park. He owns a mansion, which I expected, considering he probably makes more money than I do, and I make a hefty amount. The driveway looks like it was freshly paved, and the grass is so green it looks fake, but based on the softness of it on my shoes, it's real. Flowers line up along the house in all colors, pink, red, orange, yellow, and purple. The house has a light white-wash brick exterior, creating a vintage but rich vibe to it. Honestly, the whole house looks fake and picture-perfect.

I walk up to the door and knock loud enough so he can hear me. After a few minutes, the door opened and I completely stopped breathing, blinking, and thinking. The person standing in front of me should not be at this house. She should be far from it.

"Angelina? What the fuck are you doing here?" I ask.

The look on her face shows that she is just as shocked as I am. She looks behind her and then walks out, quietly shutting the door behind her.

"I'm having dinner with my parents. Why are you here?" she asks back.

No, no, no. Please, God, no.

Inhale, exhale. Inhale, exhale.

I close my eyes and ask the question that's haunting my thoughts. "Angel. What's your father's name?"

She looks confused but goes on.

"Lorenzo Vittori."

You've got to be kidding me. She never told me her last name, or I would've made the connection. He never mentioned a daughter. I bring my hands up to my face and groan in frustration. This is so bad. As if it couldn't get worse, Enzo opens the door. He immediately knows something is going on if I'm showing up at his house.

I look at him. "You weren't answering your phone. We need to talk."

Even though all I want to do is take Angelina far away from here, I have to address the matter at hand first.

"Come in. I turned my phone off to have dinner with my family, but it must be urgent if you went through all this trouble," he says calmly, not noticing the connection between me and his daughter.

He leads me to his office, and I see a glimpse of a pink room on the way there. I want nothing more than to look inside, but I keep walking. He can't find out I know Angelina, at least not yet. He closes the office door, and I focus on business manners.

"One of the employees lost a guy last night. He was beaten to the edge of death but managed to escape when the dumb fuck left the room. He's been fired," I say.

"Jesus. Can't trust anyone to finish the job anymore. Fucking idiot. I'll make some calls and get on the phone with Rocco. He can get the authorities off our back. In the meantime, I'll find the guy myself and take care of it," he reassures me.

I nod my head in agreement. Enzo doesn't care for small talk and never has. He gets straight to business, and then once that's finished, you leave.

He motions at the door for me to leave, but right before I walk out of the office, I ask the question that's been on my mind since I got here.

"Why didn't you tell me you had a daughter?" I ask carefully.

He looks up, and I can see in his eyes that this is a sensitive subject. I'm walking on thin ice but won't leave until I get an answer.

He shrugs and says, "Never asked."

While that may be true, I feel like he isn't being honest. I couldn't find Angelina anywhere after I met her. There was no social media, no attendance in any of the nearby schools, no public knowledge of her—nothing. It was like she was hidden.

Knowing he won't give me more information, I leave and close the office door.

I look around and quickly sneak into the pink room, curiosity eating me from the inside out. It looks like a room for a three-year-old, but I know it's Angelina's, considering the other rooms around the house look empty. A bed and canopy are in the corner, as well as a desk and a closet. There's not much else, and it's kind of depressing. Don't bedrooms usually have decorations, pictures, or anything? This doesn't look like Angelina at all, and it frustrates me that she lived such a sad childhood.

I know what a home should look like. It shouldn't be as picture-perfect as the exterior of this house looks, the rooms shouldn't be empty, and Angelina's room shouldn't be so bland. When I was a little boy, and my parents were still alive, my room was full of life. I had a race car bed, blue walls with glow-in-the-dark stars on the ceiling, and all kinds of toys scattered on the floor. My room and childhood home were welcoming

regardless of my parents' criminal life.

I begin to walk down the spiral staircase but stop when I

see who must be Enzo's wife in the kitchen. I've never seen her

before. Enzo is always alone when I see him and doesn't

typically go on public outings.

His wife has blonde hair like Angelina's, but it's curly

and cut short, hitting right above her shoulders. She looks to be

in her late forties and has some defined lines along her face and

skin. She's so skinny her health should be questioned. I may be

in a whole other room, but I could spot the purple bags under her

eyes from a mile away. She's zoned out, and looks sad and

hollow inside, almost lifeless.

I leave her in peace and make my way to the other side

of the house, desperate to find Angelina before Enzo's finished. I

should have a good hour or two before he comes out of the

office, but I won't push my luck. I find her by the front door, where I last saw her. She's just standing there in shock. I come up behind her and put one hand on her hip and the other on her mouth so she doesn't make a sound. I motion her toward an empty room where her parents won't come looking. We make it to a dark, deserted living room and hide in the corner.

I whisper in her ear, "I'm going to take my hand off of your mouth and explain everything, but you have to promise to be quiet."

She nods, and I remove my hand. She speaks quietly and obeys like the good girl I know she is.

"I don't understand. Why are you here, Nico, and why were you speaking to my father?" she asks with worry in her voice.

I tell her the truth. "Your father is my business partner. He has been for years. He never mentioned a daughter, so I had no idea you even existed."

"Business partner?" She asks, clearly confused.

Now, that caught me off guard. I figured she knew a little about what he does for work. "You don't know?"

She shakes her head, and honestly, I shouldn't be surprised. Enzo is not the type to share his dark secrets with anyone.

"If I tell you, you cannot tell anyone. I mean it. If you do, it could get us both killed," I say.

I look into her eyes to make sure she understands.

I go on. "The club isn't my only source of income. I'm a gambler in the mafia and your father is my partner."

I can see her mind racing in a million different directions.

She starts the questions off slowly. "So, my father is a gambler too?"

I don't want to hurt her with the truth, but I won't lie to her either. "Baby. Your father isn't in the mafia for gambling. More like… Making people disappear."

Her eyes bulge, and she no longer talks at an inside voice level. "Oh my god! My father's a murderer!"

I cover her mouth and back her up to the wall before she raises attention. The last thing we need is for her father to come down the stairs and see us together or have a meet-and-greet with her mother.

I try to calm her, "Shhh. Only to people who deserve it. People you don't want on the streets, trust me."

She still looks angry and a bit hurt, so I keep talking. If she gets in her head, she'll spiral.

I add, "I didn't know about you, you have to believe me. Knowing he did this to your face, I can't…" I lightly brush the faint bruise with my thumb up to her cheek. She pulls back like I struck her.

Her voice comes out clipped and serious. "How did you know it was him?"

"I saw his text the night I put you to sleep," I confess.

She scoffs, "Oh, so now you are reading my texts?"

Okay, this is getting out of hand. "No. Just the one."

"Nico, you can't just go around reading people's texts. There's this thing called priv—"

I kiss her before she loses all sanity. Don't get me wrong, I love her voice, but she's getting in her head and questioning my intentions, and I don't want her to think that way about me. Plus I wanted to kiss her the moment she opened the front door.

Just because I was shocked doesn't mean my need for her weakened.

I kiss her ferociously; I missed her so fucking much. She opens her mouth to me, and I groan. I shove my tongue through hers and pick her up by the backs of her thighs. She moans when she feels my erection against her middle. I bite her earlobe, kiss her neck, and then glide my tongue from the bottom of her neck up to the top. Right when I start to move and grind against her, she shoves at my chest and breaks the kiss.

She wipes her lips as if she can take back the kiss. "I will not be my father's partner's whore."

"You think I'm still going to work with him after he hit you? Not a chance," I say.

"What are you saying?" She asks.

"I'm saying I need a new partner, and I know just who could do the job," I say with a wink.

She pauses and then starts laughing, but I'm not amused.

Her voice is still full of humor when she speaks. "Nico, you can't be serious."

I cross my arms and raise an eyebrow.

She shakes her head and says, "No. I will not be your new murderer. Not happening. I refuse to be my father."

"I can handle that part of the job. Angelina, you can do this. There's no one I'd rather have by my side. I'll train you to be the best mafia boss out there," I do my best to convince her.

She contemplates it, and to be honest, I did too at first. I knew I needed to replace her father the moment I found out who he was. I will not have a piece of shit daughter-beater as my partner. Most people would find me ludicrous for thinking a woman can be mafia, but most women aren't her. I see potential in her.

Angelina is innocent and pure, but deep down she keeps hidden parts of her. I see the ruthless, strong parts she keeps locked away; I see all of her. I can train her to defend herself in situations that I can't. I want my girl to be protected at all costs, and I can't be around her twenty-four-seven with a business to run and gambling to keep up with. I will train her to be my equal in the mafia, the Bonnie to my Clyde.

She cowers. "Fine. But I better get paid well."

Leave it to my girl to make demands.

I smirk. "Of course. I'd expect nothing less for mio angelo."

CHAPTER 13

Angelina

I told myself I'd never set foot anywhere near my father's vicinity again, but my soft spot for my mother won the argument after she begged me to come home for dinner. A part of me believes my father connived her into begging. He knew I wouldn't listen to him. I may have agreed to this dinner, but only with demands in place: no electronics, no work, no fighting, just a normal family dinner. That was asking too much, considering Nico showed up.

After Nico left, I waited for my father to come back downstairs for hours, but he never did. He stayed up in his office all evening. I wanted a simple dinner, just one in my whole eighteen years. I understand that there was an emergency to take care of, but why does it have to take the whole night? My mother remained in the kitchen the entire time, and I think I heard her crying at one point. She does that often, but only when my father's not in the room. The sight of her baking in the kitchen brings me back to the old times, the good times with my mother. Before she was closed off and distant.

"Great job, sweetie!" my mom shouts with pride.

I look up at my mom with the biggest smile on my face. I love it when she smiles too. She kisses the top of my head, which she can barely reach even with me on the footstool. I can't reach the counter yet, but one day I will be able to!

We're baking strawberry cupcakes for my third birthday. I begged for a birthday party, but my daddy refused. I may not get a party, but my momma got me cupcake mix at the store, which makes me happy. She said not to tell Daddy though. He doesn't like messes.

We finish mixing the dough in the bowl, and I hear the oven beep in the background. My momma showed me how to put the liners in, and then I started to pour the mixture into the cups.

I can smell the sweet strawberry dough coming from the bowl, and it makes me excited to taste it. The counter around me is a mess of powder and raw dough, and I dropped a cracked egg on the floor earlier. My momma dips her finger in the bowl of pink dough and then licks it off with a smile.

"Delicious!"

That makes me giggle. I do the same with my finger, and it does taste yummy like sugar and fruit.

My momma doesn't spend time with me often. I usually just play in my room alone. But she asked me if I wanted to make cupcakes with her for my birthday, and I was so happy that I hopped up and down until I ran out of breath and my legs ached.

I'm almost done putting the dough in the cups when I hear the door slam shut from another room. My momma and I *stop what we're doing. Her smile disappears when I look up at her, and she looks terrified.*

"Sweetie, go to your room. Mommy has to talk to Daddy."

She grabbed me under my shoulders and put me on the ground. I ran out of the kitchen quickly, not wanting my daddy to see me. But I didn't go to my room; I went to the stairs above, where I could still hear their voices. I want my momma to be okay.

"Honey, you're home early. What a nice surprise. I was just making cupcakes. They'll be done soon if you're hungry—"

My momma rambles on a lot when she's nervous.

"What the fuck is this?" my daddy screams.

My body jerks when I hear the pans fall to the ground.

I see the cupcakes being thrown all over the kitchen walls and then feel something wet slide down my cheek.

"It's a fucking wreck in here. Do you think this is what I want to come home to after work?"

I reach my fingers up to my face to dry my tears, but they don't stop flowing. I have to hold my hand over my mouth to keep myself from sobbing and making a scene. My daddy calls me mean names when I cry. He says I'm weak and wishes they had a son who didn't act like such a baby.

My momma apologized to him a dozen times, but it didn't help. I hear a loud slap and scream. That's when I go to my room and cry in my pillow for the rest of the night. Happy birthday to me.

I wish I could say that was my worst birthday ever, but every birthday was just as bad. After that day, my mother shut me out completely. She wanted nothing to do with me. I haven't had a strawberry cupcake since.

Some days, my father acts like he cares and has moments of kindness. But it's quickly replaced by anger or the need for complete control. I would bet all of my money that he is bipolar with a dash of a temper. Okay, more than a dash.

As I'm walking out the door I feel a single tear slide down my face from the memory. I try to keep those deep down where I can't find them, but it's hard when I see, hear, or smell things that bring me back to that day. I quickly wipe the tear away, get in my car, and head towards the hotel.

I go up to my room in desperate need of some form of relief. Today was frustrating, confusing, and depressing.

I take my clothes off and then turn my shower on so hot that the steam fills the bathroom in seconds. Once I get in and feel the water scolding my skin, I take the deep breath that I've been holding. I wash my body, exfoliate, and shave every part of me. I'm about to shampoo my hair when I hear a loud knock on the door. I almost ignore it, but then another knock follows.

Impatient prick.

I squeeze the excess water out of my hair and grab the white towel on the rack, quickly wrapping it around my body. For this being such a luxurious hotel, their towels are teeny. It just barely covers me up. Water is all over the floor as I walk to the door. A third set of knocking occurs, and this one is more annoying than the last two.

"Wha—" I yell.

I shut my mouth when I yank the door open and see who is standing there.

"Bout time mio angelo."

He looks me up and down and takes in my current wardrobe.

His voice drops to a dangerous tone. "Is this how you always answer the door?"

I add sarcastically, "Well, when someone's about to break my door with their fist, I don't have much of a choice except to stop what I'm doing, do I?"

He looks over my shoulder at the steam coming from the bathroom, which is now filling up my room.

"Why are you here, and how did you find out where I'm staying?" I ask.

"My credit card notified me of the hotel bill. I'm here because you're not answering my texts or calls."

"I was driving, and then I wanted a shower when I got back to the hotel. Oh, I'm sorry. Next time, should I send you my daily itinerary?" I say with attitude.

I don't think he's a fan of my tone. He invites himself in, and I just stand there in shock. I scoff and then slam the door. He's seated on the couch, clearly making himself comfortable in my temporary home. I shake my head at his arrogance.

"Feel free to finish your shower. I'll wait."

I guess I never really looked at him until now, too blinded by my dramatics. He's dressed in black dress pants and a white button-up. His muscles fill in the sleeves of his shirt snugly, showing off his toned arms. His tattoos are so dark that I can see them through the white fabric. His hair is perfectly gelled back, and I have to refrain from the urge to mess it up. He watches me like I'm watching him. His eyes go from my toes to my dripping legs, to my breasts that are barely contained by the towel. I didn't have time to dry off, so I'm dripping water all over the floor. The room gets hot, but I can't tell if it's from the steam or his presence. He stands up and walks toward me slowly. My breathing goes shallow.

I feel a droplet of water run its way from my hair to my neck. It's about to go down my breasts and under the towel, but

Nico stops it with his finger. The simple touch makes me suck in a breath.

As I lick my lips, he tracks the movement of my tongue.

His voice is strained when he speaks. "What are you waiting for?"

Funny, I'm wondering the same thing. The shower didn't bring me the relief I craved, so I did something I'll probably regret. I drop the towel around my body, and his hands ball into tight fists at his sides. He stares at it on the ground, then slowly lifts his eyes to me.

"You," I smirk.

CHAPTER 14

Nicolai

She turns around and walks toward the shower, *naked.* Every inch of her is breathtaking. I had a hard-on the second I opened the door to her in a towel that barely covered her body, and now my cock is raging against my pants. As much as I loved seeing her in nothing but a towel, I was beyond pissed that she opened the door like that. I could've been anyone, and only I get to see her like this. When she dropped the towel, there was nothing left to imagine. My hard-on is painful at this point, and it needs relief like a drug addict needs coke.

I walk toward the steam while unbuttoning my shirt, but I don't get in the shower with her yet, despite how much I want to. My shirt is gone, but I leave my pants on. My back leans against the sink counter, with my arms crossed, watching her. She doesn't look my way, but she knows I'm here. I watch as the water flow drips down her perfectly round tits and then down to her ass. I can tell the water is scolding by the way it changes her body to the shade of her lips. I'm starving for a taste of her. It's killing me slowly, not touching her, but I want to keep my control in check. I'm refraining from what my body demands, but only momentarily. I grip the sink countertop behind me, and my knuckles turn white from how hard I'm holding onto my control. She tilts her head back and moves her hands up to her tits to grab them. That's when my control snaps.

When I get in the shower, the water burns my skin, but I love it. I grab both her wrists when she tries to touch herself and push her against the tile. Not enough to hurt but enough to restrain her from her actions. She gasps, and the sound makes my cock twitch. I lick the side of her neck up to her earlobe and then lightly bite, causing her to jolt.

"That's for opening the door nearly naked. Do that again, and the bite will bleed," I say in a tone that is anything but kind.

She runs her hand down my chest full of ink, and I can see her eyes taking in each tattoo. She gets to my pants, which are soaked from the shower. I could've taken them off before I stepped in, but I wasn't willing to wait a second longer. She starts to undo them, and I let her. She moves them down my legs and remains on her knees once they're discarded. She looks up at me, and her mouth is inches from my cock. The view of her red skin, steam surrounding us, water dripping all over her body, and lustful eyes make me want more than she's willing to give. I want all of her. Every single part. I want to claim her as mine, over and over again. She's about to wrap her mouth around my cock, but I grab her hair and pull her up. Trust me I've been dying for her mouth on me like that, but it's not enough. She stands, and I stop doing what I want, and instead do what I need.

"I need to taste you," I plead.

She nods her approval.

I grab her by her thighs, pick her up so she's wrapped around my waist, and sit her on the ledge in the shower. The shampoo and body wash bottles go flying, but I don't give two fucks. I get on one knee, spread her legs, and then look up into her eyes.

"Mio," I claim what's mine.

She sighs with impatience. "Make me wait any longer, and I'll find someone else to do the job."

I bite the inside of her thigh for that comment and her back arches. I put my hands on her knees to keep her legs wide open and then lick from her thigh to her aching pussy. She's soaked, but not because of the water pouring over us.

I never knew I was this hungry until I tasted her. I've been starved and deprived of what's mine, and I won't ever go without a taste again. I look up at her from between her legs and see that her eyes are closed, with her teeth sinking in her lip.

That won't do. I pinch her clit, and her body jumps.

"Look at me and open that pretty mouth. I want to see and hear what I do to you," I demand.

Once she's obeyed, I lean down to continue. I lick her fast and slow at both paces so she's on the edge of finishing. She grabs a fist full of my dripping wet hair and pulls, forcing my mouth off of her. I look up, and the view of her unraveling because of me is fucking astonishing.

"I need more," she moans breathlessly.

Greedy little thing.

"Where are your manners, mio angelo?"

"Please, Nico. I want all of you," she begs.

I grab her by the back of her thighs and pick her up. I pin her against the glass shower door, with my cock inches from inside her. I put my lips to her ear.

"You may be mio angelo, but I'm il tuo diavolo," I whisper.

I slam into her, making it fit, and she screams in both pain and pleasure from the stretch.

"Fuck you feel so good, baby," I groan.

I fist her hair, and her head jerks back, exposing her neck. I kiss her lightly to ease her pain, and then suck, leaving hickeys. *I'm not afraid to mark what's mine.*

She starts moving against my slow pace, desperate for more.

"Please, Nico," she begs.

"Good girl." Her manners are exquisite today.

I fuck her at a faster, harder pace. But I can tell she still needs more, so I give her what she wants. The only reason I know what that is is because I want it, too. I move one hand up to her neck and apply pressure. Her hands move to my back, and her red nails scratch across. I can feel them scratch deeper, leaving marks. We both inflict pain on each other amid pleasure, and it couldn't be any more fucking euphoric.

She grabs my shoulders and starts sliding in and out of my cock quicker, taking control of me. Her tits bounce in my face, and I can't resist the urge, so I take one in my mouth and bite lightly. It sends her over the edge, and she's screaming my name so loud the whole hotel can probably hear. I look down at her pussy crying for me and see a hint of blood. *Oh, sweet Jesus, I popped her cherry.* Knowing that no one else has been inside of her makes me explode inside of her as she orgasms around my cock. I've never finished in anyone before, always sure to use a condom. I loved the thought of filling her with my cum, so that's exactly what I did.

"Holy fuck, angel. I'll never get enough of you," I say with barely any breath left.

I slowly slide out of her and put her down. She almost topples over, so I grab her waist to balance her.

"I'm not on birth control, Nico."

"I don't give a flying fuck. Now turn around so I can clean you up," I order.

She turns her back to me, and I lather her hair with coconut-scented shampoo. I massage her scalp and sneak some kisses on her shoulder while I do so. She moans and relaxes. The sound makes my dick twitch, but I don't want to hurt her with round two, so I ignore the urge. I brush conditioner through her hair next and then lather her in body wash. The soap smells like vanilla honey, and it's the sweetest sensation. I clean every inch of her, from head to toe. Then, quickly do the same to me. I shut the shower off, step out, grab her towel, and wrap it around her. Then dry me off next.

I didn't bring any extra clothes, and I was not expecting to stay the night, so I only put on my boxers. She wears nothing but my white button-up that barely covers her ass, and I love how it looks on her way more than it does me. I fell asleep not long after we laid down with my arm around her waist, my face in her hair, and the smell of coconuts sending me into the sweetest slumber.

CHAPTER 15

Angelina

I tried making Nico breakfast this morning, but he insisted on eating me instead of the bacon and eggs I made. *Not that I'm complaining.*

Nico fucked me yesterday, and to be honest, it hurt at first. I thought he was too big for me, but his light kisses and sensual touches made me relax, and eventually, he fit perfectly. The sex was so good I'm worried we will never stop, and at that rate, I'll be pregnant before I can blink. I advised him to pull out next time and he agreed but only after I agreed to swallow every time he does.

I look at my phone, and a few messages pop up.

Rosie: You busy today?

Gia: I miss you already. Let's hang out.

Father: I'm sorry about dinner the other night. It was a work emergency, and I had no choice.

Nico walks up behind me, and I show him my texts.

"You're welcome to go with your friends. Or you can start your training today. After all, you don't become a mafia boss in the blink of an eye," his voice is full of sincerity. He doesn't push me to start training, nor does he push my friends away, and I appreciate that more than he knows.

I contemplate my options but go with what I want. I'm finally out of my father's chokehold so I'm going to be as selfish as I can be. Right now, I want to train with Nico.

"You have me at your mercy," I add.

Poor choice of words? Likely, considering a devilish grin spreads across his face.

Nico drives us back to his place to start the training. Is it normal to be nervous and excited at the same time? I want nothing more than to be at Nico's side as his partner, but I'm not as good as my father. I don't know what he was like at work, but I know he puts his job first before everything. Making him way more skilled and experienced than me.

The thing is, when I look at Nico, all of those thoughts and doubts about not being good enough disappear. I can see his faith in me; it's as clear as day. He truly believes I can do this, so I do, too.

I wish I could be one of those people who are like, but he's still my father and all, but I'm not. After he hit me, my soft spot for family was small, barely existent. I gave him a chance to make up, and he crushed it by making work his priority over family.

We pull into Nico's house, and my mouth goes dry. It's smaller than the house I grew up in, but nicer. It's completely black on the outside, three stories high, and the driveway is big enough to fit a dozen cars. There are a few large windows, but they're all so tinted and dark that they almost blend with the exterior. It's secluded from everything, without any nearby houses or shops.

"You own all of this?" I ask.

"Yep. So do you. What's mine is yours," he says as if it's that simple. It is as if the rate at which our relationship is moving isn't fast enough.

A sarcastic laugh passes my lips as I say, "You don't even know me. The first time we met, I stole from you."

"I'm aware and very impressed, might I add. No one has ever stolen from me and lived to see the next day. I didn't catch you in the act; you got away with it. That's mafia potential," he says.

We go inside, and his house is stunning. It could use some décor and color, but otherwise, it's gorgeous. It's very modern and classy. It has a dark vibe, but I'd expect nothing less when it comes to Nico.

A spiral black staircase to the left of the front door has a glass railing. All of the walls are black, and the floor is a shiny dark marble. It's very clean in here, and I'm not sure whether that's Nico's doing or a housemaid's. The windows on the walls are so big I could jump through them, and it's reassuring to know I couldn't see inside them when looking from the outside in. I didn't even realize I was walking around being nosy until Nico's voice jumped me out of my trance.

"Your training will be in the basement most of the time. First, follow me. As much as I love seeing you in a tee shirt and leggings, you can't wear that," he says.

I follow Nico upstairs to what I believe is his room. The master bedroom walls are red, the only color I've seen so far in his house. A king-size bed sits in the center with silky black sheets that look like heaven to sleep on. A black dresser is on the side, as well as a closet full of suits and ties. Nico walks up to me after snooping around and hands me an article of clothing.

"This is what you will wear," he says.

I grab it from his hands and examine the outfit. It's a black pantsuit but less business and more athletic. The suit is a one-piece with long sleeves, a zipper down the front, and pants connecting the outfit as one. It gives off a cat-woman vibe. It has pockets in the thighs, straps all over, buckles, and a belt with a gun holder. It's badass, and honestly, I love it. I'm speechless and in awe of a simple piece of clothing.

Nico goes to shut the door and adds, "I'll leave you to change. Come downstairs to the basement when you're ready."

He steps out of the room, and I remove my dingy clothing. I'm glad he got me this suit because I can't imagine training with my arms exposed, and wearing a paper-thin t-shirt and leggings would be safe. After a few minutes, I finally got it on. It is skin-tight but not too small and surprisingly comfortable.

I walk up to the mirror, and I'm at a loss for words. I look so different. I no longer look like a fragile little girl to be pitied but rather someone who kills mercilessly. Wearing this is like exposing a whole other side to me. A darker side. Another plus, I look hot. The suit shows off my ass and tits when I zip it down enough to show a hint of cleavage. I throw my hair up in a high ponytail and look in the mirror one last time. Something feels like it's missing, and I know exactly what that is. I dig through my purse for my red lipstick and then apply it to my lips. Much better.

I make my way down to the basement, and once I get down the stairs, I stop in my tracks to let my eyes take in the space. No wonder we're doing my training here.

On one side is a gym and boxing area. Another corner has guns hanging on the wall, from pistols to shotguns to AK-15s. There are targets by the gun wall for practicing and a table full of weaponry nearby full of throwing knives, brass knuckles, machetes, flame throwers, and the list goes on. The whole thing is intimidating, but not out of fear, more like the unknown. I don't know how to use anything in this whole room.

Nico studies my body from the bottom up and smiles. His eyes stop at my lips, and I can tell his head is full of dirty thoughts, but he doesn't act on them. We have training to focus on.

"Looking good, angel."

I do a slow spin. "Thanks. I'm quite fond of this pantsuit."

I stop mid-spin when a wall catches my eye. I know Nico is rich and highly known in the mafia, but this wall is full of enough weapons to support an army.

"Don't worry. We will start small and save the weapons for later," he says as if I'm frightened.

"They don't scare me," I say.

"Good," he says as he walks away.

He grabs a wooden chair from the corner and puts it in the center of the room.

"Sit," he orders.

I obey. I don't know what he has planned, but I have to trust him because my training is limited in time.

"Lesson number one is strategy," he says.

He walks up to me, and I have to crane my head to meet his eyes. He lifts a finger and grazes it along my cheek, the simple touch making me shiver.

"You may have the face of an angel, but you need to have the mind of a killer," he says.

I keep eye contact as he circles me slowly. He stops, moves in toward me, and leans down on the arms of the chair. His face is so close to mine that I can feel his hot breath on my lips.

"Tell me, mio angelo, how good of a liar are you?" he asks.

I quirk my eyebrow. "I lied to you, didn't I?"

He nods and says, "Fair point, but you could do better."

He stands straight and crosses his arms, making his muscles pop. *Focus, Angelina.*

His voice is firm when he speaks. "Do not hesitate when speaking a lie. That's a giveaway. Always make eye contact. Do not stutter, and speak confidently. Don't fidget with your hands, bounce your knee, or anything else. These are all tells, and people will notice them immediately. If you get caught in a lie doing mafia business, depending on what it is, it could get you killed. Understood?"

I nod.

"Good. Next, always be the quiet one. In meetings, public gatherings, with your employees, basically everywhere. Only talk when you need to. Too much talking exposes you, and you should always leave others guessing," he says.

Makes sense. "Okay, got it," I confirm.

"Last, do not even think about making friends in this business. Every single person will backstab you for their benefit. You have me and that's all you'll need," he says.

I nod. This is a lot of information at once, but I keep it in the back of my mind, making sure not to forget any of it.

He continues, "Manipulation is key in mafia, and you must master it. Beauty is dangerous, but intelligence is lethal.

Your looks will make it easier for you, but the mind games are where it's at."

"Okay, how am I supposed to do that?" I ask.

"Easy. First, there's luring, teasing, or lying. Then, you get them right where you want them and do what you deem best," he answers.

He adds, "Tease and lure whoever you want with your looks or even a good deal to do the trick, one they can't refuse. Don't go too crazy with the teasing; you're mine, and I don't share."

He winks and grips my chin, forcing me to look at him.

"Look at you, angel. You can manipulate any man with just your looks and words."

He drops the hold he has on me.

"Last thing and the most important. If you take anything from this lesson, remember this," he says.

His tone is clipped and dead serious. "Do. Not. Fucking. Rat. Snitching will get you killed. Guaranteed. In a hypothetical situation, you never break, no matter how hard they push."

His eyes darken dangerously, and his voice lowers to a frightening tone.

"Is that clear?"

I swallow.

"Crystal," I reply.

He lightens up after I hold his eyes, proving to him that I understand the importance of the lesson.

"Good. Congratulations, mio angelo, you've passed the first lesson," he says proudly.

CHAPTER 16

Nicolai

She told me the weapons didn't scare her, so I took advantage of that and decided her next lesson was learning to use them. I led her over to the wall of weaponry and faced her toward my extensive collection. I crossed my arms and waited, curious about what she would do next.

"Choose," I order her.

She looks at me and then back to the wall full of options. On the matte black wall hangs daggers, throwing knives, ninja stars, a flame thrower, axes, brass knuckles, machetes, a few swords, grenades, tasers, batons, bows, and much more. I can work with anything that she chooses, but in my opinion, some of these are better than others.

She slowly walks along the wall and lightly brushes her fingers across a sword blade, then the sharp tips of the ninja stars. She picks up a few items but puts them back clearly

disinterested. She stops by the large collection of knives and

picks up a set of three. They're small, black, and tough to grip

but deadly if you know how to use them.

"I like these," she says with a small smile.

That's my girl.

She couldn't have chosen a better option. All the

weapons on this wall do damage, but it depends on who is

yielding it. She chose perfectly. The throwing knives are quick

to use and easy to hide under clothing.

"Good choice. Follow me," I say.

She's right behind me as I walk over to our target. I

move the target to the front to show her where to hit.

I go on, "Lesson two is yielding your weapon. You will

carry those knives everywhere you go. They are now yours, and you will use them if ever necessary. First, you have to learn how."

"If you could guess where to hit this target and successfully kill them, where would you say that is?"

She contemplates it momentarily and then points to the target's chest.

I shake my head in disapproval. "Wrong. Most people would agree with you, but few know the right answer, leading to the target killing them first or getting away."

I point to the neck of the target and say, "To kill, aim for the jugular. It will make your target bleed out painfully and slowly. This spot will never fail to finish the job."

She nods. I've noticed she is very observant and good at listening.

I move the target back a bit further and grab Angelina's shoulders, guiding her to where she needs to stand. I hand her one of the black throwing knives and place her fingers on the end of it, showing her how and where she needs to hold it.

I whisper in her ear, "Hold it here, or else you'll lose grip, and the knife will not go where you want it to. Always have a tight hold on it."

I stand behind her so I can see every movement she makes. As she raises her arm, I lightly put my fingers on her elbow and then slowly move it up her forearm. She has goosebumps, and I love that I affect her this way. I pull her arm back toward the side of her face, just a few inches from her ear.

"Aim for the jugular, and never take your eyes off the spot you want to hit. Take a deep breath, and then throw straight on with full force," I say.

She inhales and exhales. I watch her eyes focus on the target, and she almost perfects every movement until my hand touches her hip. If a time comes that she has to use a knife, there will be distractions all around her. Whether those distractions are touches, sounds, or people, she needs to be able to focus solely on the target. I catch her eyes moving in my direction for a millisecond before they go back to the target. She throws it, and it lands on the target's shoulder. She may have missed the neck, but I'm proud of her for landing the knife in.

I lean down from behind her, put my lips against her hair, and whisper, "Do you know why that missed?"

She shakes her head no.

"You took your eyes off the target. Doing that for even a second will throw you off. There will always be distractions around you; you need to learn to focus regardless," I say.

"I want to try again," she says with determination.

"Very well," I say.

She positions herself, pulls out a second knife, and flicks her ponytail over her shoulder. As she does, I catch a whiff of coconut mixed with vanilla. *I'm supposed to be distracting her; what a joke. Damnit, focus, Nico.*

"Miss this one, Angelina, and I'll take you over my knee," I warn.

Her breath hitches, but she doesn't take her eyes off the target. She leans her right arm back, takes a deep breath, and throws. I follow the knife to where it lands, the center of the jugular—a perfect throw.

"Good girl. But I must admit I was hoping you'd miss," I say with a hint of playfulness.

Her cheeks turn a rosy pink, and I hear her stomach rumble.

"Lesson two passed. Now let's go get some food in your system," I smack her ass as I walk away and she giggles.

We go upstairs, and I grab some ingredients from the fridge, pantry, and spice cabinet.

She crosses her arms. Whenever she does that, she has an attitude, and I won't lie—I find it cute as hell. "I don't see how cooking will help me in the mafia business."

"It won't. Like I said, we're taking a break, and I'm making dinner for you. You can start the next lesson tomorrow," I say.

She just stands there in shock, staring at me.

"You cook?" She asks.

"Yes, I cook. I am human, you know," I smile at her.

She shrugs. "Just didn't take you as the cooking type."

I mix up my mamma's signature vodka pasta sauce. It's made of minced garlic, a diced onion, heavy whipping cream, red pepper flakes, garlic powder, Italian seasoning, rosemary, shredded parmesan, and a dash of vodka. The secret ingredient? She used fresh tomatoes from the garden and crushed them into a tomato paste rather than using the store-bought kind. Trust me, it makes a difference.

I inhale the aroma coming from the pot, and I feel like I'm flashed back in time, playing with my toys as the house is full of the signature sauce smell. I turn around as I hear my mamma's faint voice.

"Oh, my sweet boy, dinner is ready! Tutti a tavolo a mangiare!" My mamma yells.

I'm so stuck in my trance, clinging to the memory of my mamma, that I don't even hear Angelina repeating my name until she shakes my shoulders. A single wet tear slides down my cheek, but I brush it off before she notices. Sometimes, the memory of a loved one is all you have left of them, so you're stuck clinging to it like they never left you in the first place.

"Nico? Are you okay?" She asks with worry.

"Yeah. Sorry, I zoned out," I reassure her.

I turn around and gather a spoonful of sauce, blow on it, and walk over to Angelina.

"Open," I order.

She opens her mouth wide as I bring the spoon into her mouth.

She moans, and the sound goes straight to my dick.

Her eyes bulge. "Holy fuck. How did you make this sauce?"

"Mamma's recipe. Sorry, I promised not to tell," I say as I hold my hands up in surrender.

"Well, in that case, when can I meet her? That's the best sauce I've ever tasted."

I look away, unable to meet her eyes. I stir the sauce to distract myself from talking about something I typically hide from others. It's hard to talk about losing my parents. Saying it aloud reminds me that I'm living in a world without the two people I love most.

"You can't. Both my parents died when I was younger."

"Oh, Nico, I'm so sorry."

She puts her hand on my bicep and moves it up and down to comfort me. I wouldn't say I like comfort, taking it as pity. But with Angelina, it doesn't feel that way. For once, it feels genuine.

"What happened?" she asks.

This is usually where I shut down and kick the woman out, but this girl is different. I want to tell her everything about me and be an open book. She makes me want to be vulnerable for a change.

I lay my heart out to her. "They were murdered, and the killer is still out there. It eats me alive every waking day, and whenever I get a lead, it ends up being a dead end. I joined the mafia to find the fucker who did it."

She moves her hand from my bicep, puts herself between me and the saucepan, and places both palms on my face, forcing me to look into her eyes.

"They won't get away with this. You have me now, and we will find them together and make them suffer," she's serious. There isn't even a hint of hesitation in her voice or eyes.

Hearing her say that she wants the same vengeance for my parents as I do urges me to send a silent prayer. I've never been a believer in religion after what was taken from me, but if there's a chance it keeps this woman on Earth with me, then fuck, I'll believe in anything.

Dear God, if you exist and you're listening to my thoughts, please never take this angel away from me. I am falling in love with her, and I can't bear to lose anyone else I love. I am a fucking fool for this woman. Apologies for the cursing, but I am. If you even consider taking her, take me first. Because I refuse to live without this angel in my life. You have plenty up there; you don't need mine, too. Amen.

I gently kiss her forehead and get back to finishing dinner. I would love nothing more than to fuck her right here on the countertop and show her how appreciative I am of her, but right now, she needs to be taken care of.

I cook bowtie shells and add spinach and mushrooms to the sauce for extra substance. Once the pasta is finished, I scoop out two bowls full and sit one in front of her.

"Eat," I order.

"Thank you, Nico."

Remind me to reward her later for those manners.

She eats the entire bowl and moans the whole time. I think I would have rather been knifed in the jugular than sit here listening to those sounds, refraining from taking her as mine.

CHAPTER 17

Angelina

I fell asleep by Nico's side last night as soon as I laid down. I was exhausted and extremely full of dinner. That was seriously the best meal I've ever had.

When Nico opened up about his parents, it was my first time seeing his soft side. My heart hurts for him, but I honestly feel more rage than sympathy. I can see how badly he wants justice for his family, and it pisses me off that the killer got away with it. I didn't know Nico's parents, but based on the man he is, they didn't deserve that fate. I told him I'd help find who did it, and I meant that.

I packed plenty of clothes but slept in one of Nico's button-up shirts. It was surprisingly comfortable and smelled like him, so I disregarded my pajamas. I grab my phone buzzing from the nightstand. We thought of the "fuck bitches get money" name on a very drunk night all together and haven't changed it since.

FBGM Group Chat

Rosie: Girl, are you ALIVE?!

Gia: She's alive, just busy railing mystery man.

Rosie: I second that theory!

Angelina: I'm fine, you psychopaths! I told you his name is Nico.

Gia: HA! She didn't deny it. I'm so right.

Rosie: We miss you :(

Angelina: Miss you both more. Please, don't befriend me for my absence. I promise I'll make it up to you with a shopping spree soon!

Gia: Deal!

Rosie: We would never befriend you. It's us three until the day I die.

Angelina: Ugh, I love you both so much.

Gia and Rosie: Love you more!

Ever since we became friends when one of us says love you, the other two of us say love you more in unison. It's like our thing, and while it is cheesy, it always warms my heart.

I miss them so much, but I have to set my priorities straight. Right now, my number one priority is partnering with Nico and becoming the best, strongest version of myself. We go back down to the basement for training, and I have no idea what Nico has planned for me. I tried getting the information out of him, but he wouldn't budge.

"Stand in the middle of the room," he orders.

I obey and wait for further instructions. He walks up behind me and drapes a black tie around my eyes, completely darkening my vision.

I cross my arms. "Nico, I don't see how this is productive."

"Lesson three, always be aware of your surroundings," he says.

I gasp when I feel a sharp, cold metal moving up my arm.

"What am I holding?" He asks.

"A knife," I answer.

He makes a disapproving sound. "Not good enough. Be specific, mio angelo."

"One of my three black, thin throwing knives," I say.

"Good. The next guesses won't be as easy, I was just warming you up," he says.

The knife leaves my arm, and the room is so quiet I could hear a pin drop. I'm nervous and on edge without my eyesight.

I hear a *click* sound in the distance but can't exactly tell what it is or where it came from.

"What was I doing, and what side of the room was I on?" he asks.

His voice is distanced, but I can hear it more clearly on the right side of me.

"Right side of the room," I answer.

"Good. Now answer the other question."

Shit. I don't know what it was. It was so faint and lasted for less than a second.

"I don't know," I say.

Click Click.

I jump. The sound was so close to my ear that I could reach out and touch it. Then the answer hits me.

"You cocked your gun," I answer confidently.

"Good girl. If you ever hear that sound, you prepare to fight or hide. They're cocking it to shoot you. Now, I'm going to walk around the room. When I say so, you'll point to where you think I am standing," he says.

I nod and quiet my breathing.

I hear his footsteps go farther and farther away. They're so quiet now I can't tell where he is.

"Point," he orders from somewhere off in the distance.

Based on his voice and where I last heard his footsteps, I guess and point to the left side of the room. I gasp, and my heart rate skyrockets out of shock and fear when a rough hand grabs my jaw and turns my head to the side.

"Wrong. I was behind you. Pay attention. You need to know where your enemy is at all times. Right now, I am your enemy," he says coldly.

I hear his footsteps again, and this time, I clear my head of all distracting thoughts. I hold my breath and don't move an inch. His footsteps stop.

"Point," he orders.

I move my finger where I believe the basement stairs are and then slightly point up.

"Very good," he praises.

His footsteps grow louder, and I hear him put something behind me.

"Last test. Sit down," he orders.

I back up slowly until I feel the chair and carefully sit on it, making sure not to fall on my ass.

He grabs my wrists and puts them behind my back. Then I feel something tie them together, rope maybe? It must be based on the scratchy friction I feel against my skin.

He pulls tightly, and it hurts, but I know it'd be way worse if this were real, so I don't complain.

"Find a way out," he orders.

I wiggle my wrists, but they don't budge even a little. If anything, the movement makes it worse.

He adds, "You can go around to find something to help you, but if you're in this situation, you need to be discreet. Do not leave the chair unless you're certain there's no one in the room with you. Don't get caught because you're impatient or scared."

Being blindfolded doesn't make this any easier, but I remember my surroundings before he took away my eyesight. The punching bag and gym equipment should be to the left of the chair. Behind me is the gun wall, and to my right is the weaponry. I slowly stand and walk toward the right to avoid tripping or running into anything. When I feel my thigh bump into a table, I stop. I turn around, pushing my back against the

table to use my hands even though they're tied. I feel around the

surface, looking for an object to help me. There's something

round, likely a grenade which I don't want to fuck with. I move

over more and feel something too heavy to help me. I stand on

my tip toes and move my hand up, which hurts my wrists,

straining against the rope and shoulders from the stretch, but I

have no choice. I feel the tip of something sharp. I grab it by the

grip so I don't slice my hand open. I turn it around so that the

sharp side faces the rope and start moving it back and forth. It's

not easy in this position, but eventually, I feel the rope loosen

and fall to the ground. I grab my wrists and rub at the burn.

They're in pain but also relief from being freed.

"Good work. It's highly unlikely that there will be a

weapon wall in this situation, and your feet will probably be tied

too, so try your best with whatever you can find or do," he says.

I go to take the blindfold off, and Nico's deep voice stops me.

"Did I say you could take that off?"

"You said that was the last test."

"It was. You passed lesson three, but I'm not done with you or the blindfold," he says.

His footsteps halt right before me, and I feel his finger lift my chin slightly. My mouth parts at his gentle touch.

"Good girls get rewards, mio angelo," he praises.

He kisses my neck, and my head tilts to the side, giving him more access to my exposed skin.

I still can't see anything which is frustrating but also a big turn-on. Only being able to feel, touch, and hear magnifies the effect compared to normal. He grabs my hand and pulls. I follow him slowly until he comes to a halt. He pulls harder this time making me stumble between his legs. I feel his shoulders below me, meaning he's sitting in the chair I was in earlier. His legs are parted, and his rough hands move up the back of my thighs, raising goosebumps to my skin.

"What do you want your reward to be? Hm?"

"You. I want it to be you," I say.

He groans.

"You'll always have me, mio angelo. No one gets me, but you and no one gets you either. Ever test that theory again, and you'll face the consequences."

I grip his shoulders and slide my hands down them to the hem of his tee shirt. I lift his shirt over his head and feel his bare chest, from the hard ridges of his abs to his strong biceps to the thick veins on his forearms. I grab the top of the chair as a guide and move to sit on his lap. I feel his erection against my cunt, and a slight moan escapes my lips. His hands move up my thighs and then grip my hips tightly.

"Do whatever you want, angel. I'm at your mercy," he says.

The power he's giving makes me step way out of my comfort zone. I step back and slowly unzip my training suit, teasing him and torturing him. Removing it without eyesight was surprisingly easy when you do it with confidence. Once my suit is thrown to the side, he sees that I wasn't wearing a bra or panties underneath, and I stand completely bare to him.

His voice comes out tortured. "Fucking bellissima."

I can't see how he's looking at me, but I can hear his heart beating rapidly. I grip his shoulder with one hand and the other a handful of his hair. As I start grinding against him, his hands move from my thighs to my ass. His fingers grip my sides so roughly that they'll leave bruise marks by tomorrow, but I don't mind. I can't see what he's doing until I feel it, which makes it more exciting when he takes my mouth into his. He thrusts his tongue into me, impatient and demanding. I move my hands over to his chest as he ravages my mouth, and I scrape my nails over his skin, leaving red scratches in my wake. I moan into his mouth, needing more.

"I want you to see what you do to me," he says against my lips.

He unties the knot on the tie covering my eyes and removes it. He's looking at me like he wants to eat me alive, and right now, I would let him.

My eyes move down to his chest, and I gasp, but not from scratch marks I left. He has small angel wings tattooed on the top left of his chest, about the size of a baseball. I know for a fact those were not there when we first met, or even last night, for that matter. I stop moving and look up at his eyes.

"Nico. When did you get this?" I ask.

He shrugs like it's no big deal. "This morning while you slept in."

"What. Why? How?" I ask with panic.

He cocks his head. "For you, of course. Problem, mio angelo?"

I slap his chest and shout at him. "It's permanent!" I laugh. "We're not even dating, for fuck's sake."

His grin disappears, and his eyes darken to a dangerous shade. I realize I said something I shouldn't have. He lifts me off of his lap.

"Bend over," he demands.

"Nic—" He cuts me off before I can finish my sentence.

"Do not make me repeat myself."

His tone is terrifying, but I can't deny that the edge to it makes me want him more.

I bend over his lap, and his fingers lightly trace my ass. It's gentle until it isn't. He slaps, and a gasp leaves my mouth.

"We're not dating? Really? You've been mine since the moment you walked into my club. That's for thinking you don't belong to me."

The aftermath of the slap burns, but he lightly caresses it afterward, and it eases the pain. I feel my arousal from how turned on I am. I won't lie; I do enjoy a tad bit of pain mixed with pleasure.

"Do not move or I'll do that again," he warns.

I remain completely still, while he moves out from under me. I put my hands on the chair to hold me up, but I don't dare to move from the bent-over position I got myself into. He moves behind me, wraps a handful of my hair in his fist, and pulls my head back toward his lips.

"Look at you, you're dripping. All for me, huh baby?"

"Please, Nico," I beg.

"Such good manners," he says.

He thrusts into me from behind without warning, and a loud moan escapes my lips. He moves in and out, driving me over the edge of sanity.

"You"—*thrust*—"are"—*thrust*—"mine."

"Yes," I moan.

"Say it," he demands.

"I'm yours."

"Whose?" he asks.

"Yours, Nicolai."

His pace moves quicker, and my eyes roll to the back of my head. He feels so good inside of me, too good. I turn my head to look into his eyes as he fucks me from behind.

"Harder. I want all of you, Nico. Don't hold back with me," I say.

He pulls out and immediately flips me so my back is on the concrete floor. His body towers over me. He lifts my leg and slams inside of me. It is ungentle, unkind, and unraveling me completely. It's what I needed, what I craved. I thrive in the animalistic, carnal side of him.

I scream in pleasure over and over as he fucks me roughly. My back aches from the floor, and my pussy burns from the stretch of his size, but fucking hell, I love it.

"Am I hurting you, angel?" He asks, but not with worry in his voice, more like a challenge.

"Yes," I moan.

"Good," he says.

He slows his pace, leans down, and licks from my stomach to my nipple. My back arches off of the concrete when I feel his teeth clamp down on one of my breasts. His tongue slides up to my neck right as his pace changes from loving back to fucking. He fucks my mouth as he fucks my cunt, and I bite his lip, something I've grown fond of doing. As his bottom lip is between my teeth, I look up at his eyes, and he grins darkly. It pulls his lips more and likely hurts against my hold, but he seems to enjoy the pain as much as I do. I remove my mouth from his, put my hands on his shoulders, and slightly lift my body from the ground, enough to meet his thrusts and take him deeper.

"Fuck," he groans.

My head tilts back, and my fingers dig into his back as I start to orgasm. It bursts through me, the sensation addicting and exhilarating. When I come down from the high, he pulls out of me and moves his dick up to my mouth.

"Swallow every drop," he orders.

I open, and his dick nearly chokes me. Warm, salty liquid shoots into my mouth, and I swallow every drop of it. When he slides out of my mouth, a drop escapes to my lips, but I dart my tongue out and lick it up.

His hand runs lightly through my hair. "Such a good girl."

Nico is bossy, terrifying, and dangerous. He's the devil himself, yet I don't run away. I can't deny my attraction for this man, and I have a feeling even if I tried to run away, he would find me. He would follow me through every lifetime, not even letting death do us part.

CHAPTER 18

Nicolai

Last night, I taught Angelina a lesson on her surroundings and another about who she belonged to. She needed to be reminded after freaking out about my new tattoo. She will be mine until the day I die. I see nothing wrong with tatting angel wings on my body.

Rocco and Enzo have called me a few times, so I texted them and told them I was taking a vacation and to leave me be all week. They weren't thrilled, but I've never taken a single day off, so they have no choice but to let it go.

I offered Angelina a break from the training, but she refused. I don't want to take her away from her friends or newfound freedom, but I can't help loving spending time with her. She still has more to learn until she's ready to step foot in the mafia world, but at this rate, she will be ready within the next few days.

Our next lesson is physical defense. Angelina is skinny and tall. She doesn't have the same strength as most mafia bosses do, as they're all men, but she has other qualities that make her better than them. At the least, I can teach her how to protect herself and predict her enemy's move.

We go down to the basement, where we've spent all our time training so far. I grab the punching gloves and slide them onto her smooth, angelic hands.

"Lesson four, physical defense and offense," I say.

"I've never used a punching bag before."

I go on, "Someday, I'll teach you to use that, but not today. You won't be punching the bag."

"Then what am I punching?"

I smirk.

She shakes her head. "No. I'll take the bag."

"Awe. Are you worried about hurting me, baby?" I ask.

She scoffs and rolls her eyes.

"I'll be fine. You can't hurt me even if you tried," I reassure her.

"Fine," she gives in.

She positions herself as if she's about to punch me, and it's cute. Awful stance, but cute.

"If you want to knock someone out cold, hit any of these spots." I point to my chin, the side of my jaw, and my temple. "If you hit hard enough, it will send a shock straight to their brain."

She nods in understanding.

"If you just want to buy some time, hit here." I point to my nose and nuts, of course.

"They'll either have to take the time and stop the blood from gushing or kneel over in pain," I tell her.

"Okay, easy enough," she says.

"If you closely watch your opponent's body language, you can see where they'll punch and block it. You need to be aware of their every move," I say.

"Now try to punch me," I order.

She takes a step forward, and I can tell where she will hit before she moves her arm. When she does punch, I grab her wrist and stop her.

"Try again," I order.

She keeps my eye contact, never looking away. She takes a step but not in the same direction as her hit. She did well, considering I couldn't predict where she was going to hit. Her punch felt like nothing, but progress is progress.

"Good hit. You catch on fast," I say.

She smiles sweetly at the affirmation. I've noticed my girl likes to be praised.

We practice throwing punches for the next four hours. I did it with her until she could predict my punches and block them, and I could no longer predict hers. She perfected every motion. Now she's sweating, panting, hungry, and exhausted.

"Lesson four complete. Go shower and clean up. I'm taking you to dinner," I tell her.

"Very bossy," she adds.

While she's in the shower, I run to town a few minutes away. I go into Saint Laurent and buy her a long grey silk dress, black heels, and deep red lipstick in which she will look stunning. I hurry home before she's done with her shower and lay the dress and heels out on the bed. I change into a grey suit to match and wait for her downstairs. She takes an hour or so to get ready, but I don't mind. I'd wait a lifetime for her.

She descends the black staircase, and my breathing stops. She's devastatingly beautiful. My gaze immediately goes to the leg slit in the dress, which exposes her smooth tan leg, and my eyes trail up her body to admire the rest. Her narrow waist and high-perched breasts hug the dress perfectly, making it look like it was made for her. Strands of honey-blonde curls tumble carelessly down her back, and her face is naturally radiant. The dark cherry-red color on her lips is my favorite part of the whole look.

I shake my head and smile.

"Tutto mio."

She comes up to me and kisses my cheek, probably marking my face with lipstick, but I don't mind one bit.

"Thank you for taking care of me. This dress and these shoes are stunning. They had to cost a fortune, Nico. You didn't have to do all this for me."

"Only a car's worth. Nothing is too expensive for my girl."

"What! Nicolai Leone, you did not spend thousands of dollars on my outfit," she says dramatically.

"I'd spend millions, fuck billions if it made you happy," I say, completely serious.

She comes closer to me and places a light kiss on my lips so all of the red doesn't transfer to me. Her forehead leans against mine with one hand in my hair.

"What did I do to deserve you?" she asks, just barely a whisper.

"No. Only I get to ask that. You deserve the fucking world at your feet. I will kiss the ground you walk on every day if that means I'm deserving of you," I say.

We walk to my car and I place a hand on her lower back. The back of the dress is exposed, and the bare skin on my hand is smooth and sexy as hell. I remove my hand to open the door for her, and then I get in next to start the car. I reach across her, pull her seatbelt out, and purposely grace my knuckles across her breasts as I buckle her in. I catch a glimpse of her hardened nipples under the silk fabric but look away before I get a hard-on. We have a reservation to get to.

"Going to tell me where we're going?"

I take her hand in mine and kiss the back of it. "Not a chance."

After thirty minutes of driving, we arrive at the restaurant. It's a rooftop steak house, with expensive, but delicious food.

"Nico, are you sure this place is open? It's empty," she says.

I laugh under my breath. "It better be, considering I spent a fortune renting it out for the evening."

Her eyes grow twice their size.

"You're kidding," she says.

I shrug my shoulders. It's not a big deal. What this girl doesn't realize is I would do anything for her. I would drain my whole bank account if it meant I could see her this happy.

This restaurant doesn't even rent out to individuals because it makes so much revenue in a day, but I offered them double what they would have made if they stayed open, and they couldn't refuse a deal like that.

"I wanted you all to myself for the night," I tell her.

"So dramatic," she says as she rolls her eyes.

"You love it."

I can tell she does based on her bright smile. We sit down at a table in the center of the roof, with a stunning view of Italy below. Candles are lit nearby, and live classical music plays in the background, creating the most peaceful sensation. Before

Angelina, I would have never gone all out for a girl like this.

I've never even taken a girl out to eat before her. Yet she

changed me, and she deserves nothing short of the best. A

waitress approaches and asks for our drink order.

"I'll take a whisky on ice and whatever she would like,"

I say.

"White wine, please."

The waitress eyes me the whole time she takes our drink

order, and it's obvious she's trying to get my attention, but I

don't look her way. Even when I ordered my drink, my eyes

were glued to Angelina, as I was in awe of her. The waitress

finally leaves when she realizes I'm not interested.

"Oh my god! Did you see her eye-fucking you?" she

scoffs. "The audacity."

My face splits into a wide grin.

"Are you jealous, angel?"

"Not at all. Just a little annoyed at the disrespect," she says.

I hum a response.

Disrespect huh?

I reach my hand out and cover her left hand with mine. My rough, calloused hands intertwine with her delicate, soft hands. The waitress approaches, still eyeing me as she does.

"Whiskey for Mr. Leone and red wine for the lady," the waitress says.

Absolutely not.

I finally meet the waitress's eyes and my glare is anything but flirtatious or kind.

"That lady is my wife, and she ordered white wine," I say.

Angelina looks at me with both shock and confusion etched on her face. I wink at her.

The waitress goes pale and gets embarrassed by me calling her out on her behavior. Her voice comes out panicked.

"I am so sorry about that, Mrs. Leone. I'll fix it right away."

She leaves in a hurry. No one disrespects Angelina, especially when I'm around.

"Wife?!" she shouts.

I shrug, it's no biggie. "She needed to show you some respect, and one day you will be."

She laughs. "You're crazy."

"For you, I'm a full-on lunatic," I tell her.

The waitress approaches again with the correct drink order and less eye-fucking.

"Have you guys made any decisions, or would you like more time?" the waitress asks.

Angelina watches me, so I order first. "I'd like the filet mignon with roasted parmesan asparagus and sweet potato fries please."

"And for you, Mrs. Leone?" the lady asks.

That's got a nice ring to it.

Angelina hands the menu to her and says, "I'll have the same, please."

After taking down our order, the waitress leaves, and it's just the two of us.

"Why do you own the club if you make plenty working for the mafia?"

I answer her the best I can. "It'd look suspicious to the public for me to be making so much money without a job. It started as a front for my financial success but I have grown to love the club and how far it has come. It started out unpopular and in low demand but is now the best club in Italy. Enough about my work, what about you? I know you want to be my partner, but is there anything else you want to do?"

She spins the wine around in her glass, contemplating her answer.

"I used to bake with my mom when I was little, and it was my favorite thing to do. We mostly just made strawberry cupcakes, but I could make other flavors if I tried. I'd like to open a cupcake bakery one day and find the joy I lost in baking again. My mother stopped baking with me after she got in trouble for the mess. After that day, I was too afraid to even step foot in the kitchen let alone bake in it."

Her eyes look sad, and I can tell she misses her passion. I will make it my life's mission to get her back in a bakery doing what she loves.

"You'll get that bakery and sell the best cupcakes in all of Italy, I promise you," I say.

We talk and eat for the rest of the evening, even long after our food is eaten. She talks about her homeschooling experience, two best friends, and everything in between. Probably because I kept asking questions and being nosy about every detail of her life. She didn't seem to mind, though. It gets dark out, and it is almost time for the restaurant to close, so I pay the check, and we go out to my black Lamborghini to head home.

"What are the odds of you letting me drive your car?" she asks.

I throw her the keys, and she catches them.

"Baby, you can do and have whatever you want when it comes to me."

She does a happy dance, and it is seriously the cutest thing I've ever seen. It makes me laugh and I feel ten years younger because of it. I haven't genuinely laughed in a long time.

She gets on the driver's side, readjusts the seat, and then turns the radio up. She looks down and pauses.

"Manual?"

"Yup. Is that a problem?" I ask.

"Nope. I may not have been allowed to drive a car, but that doesn't mean I wasted my time cooped up in my room. I watched enough videos that I should have figured it out," she says.

A part of that surprises me, but another part knows Angelina is capable of more than everyone assumes.

Her palm grips the shifter, and she leaves the parking lot smoother and faster than I drive. Seeing her control the manual transmission with such ease is dead sexy and I can't resist touching her right now, even if I tried.

That is precisely why my hand finds its way to her inner thigh. Right now, I'm very thankful for the slit down the leg of that dress, giving me easy access. My fingers move in a circular motion on her thigh, and her skin breaks out in goosebumps. She sits up and tries to squeeze her legs together, likely trying to contain her arousal.

My fingers stop moving in circles when I notice a car in the rearview mirror that's been behind us since we left the restaurant. The car is black with tinted windows so dark that I can't see who it is inside, but they've been following us for far too long to be coincidental. I can tell when someone is tailing me, and this car is.

"We're being followed. You're going to have to lose them," I say.

"What? I can't do that. I may be able to drive stick, but that doesn't mean I can race and cut corners like Nascar!" she shouts.

"You can do it. You're going to have to because we don't have time to switch places. I'll tell you what to do." I try my best to calm her down.

Her lips thin, but I don't give her time to contemplate, and she has no choice in this matter.

"You're going to have to speed up and take sharper turns. I've done it plenty of times in this car, so don't worry about flipping it."

She takes a deep breath and nods. I don't remove my hand from her thigh. While it may not have been planned, I take advantage of this opportunity for lesson five.

"Take the next left at the last second. Then speed up," I order.

She does exactly as I say. She turns sharply when it's time and quickly accelerates after she regains control. The car behind makes the turn, too, further confirming that they're on our ass.

"Faster, Angelina."

She accelerates to ninety.

I move my hand up her thigh to the edge of her panties. She tries to move out of my reach, but my palm pushes down on her thigh to keep her in place.

She huffs. "Nico, I can't focus on driving with you touching me like that."

"Too bad. Lesson five, lose a car following you," I say.

She faces me and just stares into my eyes. Her red lips part and I can't take my eyes off of her. She is the epitome of beauty.

"Eyes on the road," I remind her.

She turns her head quickly as if had forgotten she was the one behind the wheel.

"Lose the tail, angel."

She nods. She has an air of calm and self-confidence, for this being her first time driving a manual, and I devour it.

She swallows hard, lifts her chin, shifts the car, and then pushes her foot harder on the gas.

I don't give her any more instructions. She needs to lose them without my help, and I know she can. She just needs to believe it herself.

She accelerates to 120 miles per hour, and at this point, she's barely in control of the car. She takes a quick right, and the tires screech loudly as we drift into the turn. I'm fairly sure the two right wheels lifted off the ground.

She's reckless but a total badass. I couldn't be more proud.

The car behind us makes the same turn but a little slower, and we gain some distance.

I move her panties to the side and feel her slick center. *It's practically begging for me.*

She takes slow, deep breaths, and I can tell she's trying to focus despite my touch. I probably shouldn't be distracting my driver in a life-or-death, situation but I trust my girl, and I would put my life in her hands any day. I slowly drag my fingers across and then shove two inside her. They slide in like butter considering her pussy is drooling all over my car seat. I fucking love it, and this is now my favorite car out of the many I own. She moans, closes her eyes, and tilts her head back. I remove my hand and pinch her rock-hard nipples to grab her attention.

"Lose. The. Car."

Her eyes open, and she straightens with dignity. The dashboard reads 140, and she flies by other cars, signs, and stoplights. Honestly, I'm shaking in my pants, but I can't show her fear, or she'll feel it, too. There is a busy stoplight far ahead that turns from green to yellow. She accelerates even more, and the light turns red. Cars start to move, and I almost close my eyes, not wanting to see what happens, but I open them, trusting she has it handled. The cars ahead are all about to cross the intersection, but she speeds up enough to pass through them, cutting off whoever is following us. The stoplight is so busy and long that there's no way they'll get to us now. She lost the car like I knew she would.

We pull into my driveway thirty minutes later.

"Well done, baby. You passed lesson five with flying colors."

She broke into a wide, open smile. The sight of her so happy heals my heart. No literally. After my parents died, I swore to never love again, but you can't help but love a girl like her; it's inevitable. My heart shattered into a million pieces the day they were taken from me, but what Angelina doesn't realize is every day spent with her, she has been picking up piece by piece.

She leans over the center console, giving me a full view of her tits, and her red lips meet mine with pure need. We could go inside, but neither of us is willing to stop right now.

Her hand moves down from my hair to my chest, but I grab her wrist before she can go farther down. I lean forward until my lips caress her ear.

"Right now, it is all about you, not me," I say.

I slowly guide her hand up to her tits and squeeze. I brush her curls off her shoulder, kiss her collarbone and neck, and then bite her earlobe. She shudders and moans from the bite. *My girl loves my teeth.* I insert another finger inside her, making it three to fill her up. I move them slowly. While she may deserve a reward, I like to watch her completely at my mercy. I don't quicken my pace. Even when she tries to grind her body against my fingers, demanding more from me, I hold the same slow pace. I'm waiting for her to submit to me. I'm going to make sure she knows she's mine, and one of these days, she will know it too.

She makes a groaning sound, and she is, without a doubt, frustrated with me for taking my sweet old time. She's about to lose this game, and her willingness to give up so easily makes me grin devilishly.

"Use your words, baby," I demand.

She looks over at me, and her eyes are full of a desperate need for more. They're pleading for the release she craves.

"Please," she begs.

"Please, what?" I ask.

"Please, Nico."

"You're so pretty when you're begging," I tell her.

I cup her face with my free hand and kiss her deeply. Our kiss is full of tongue, smeared lipstick, and a hint of wine and whisky from dinner. It's the most delicious sensation.

I quickened my pace after she begged for it. If she keeps saying my name while I'm inside her, I'm convinced she will know who she belongs to.

At this point, she's breathless, sweaty, and devastating. As much as I'd love to see her like this all night, I can tell she's dying for release.

I fist her hair, tilt her head back, and kiss her neck all over. She tastes salty and sweet, and my cock starves for a taste of her arousal. I move my mouth down and move the fabric of her dress down to free her tits. I bite down on her nipple, and that's what sends her over the edge. She pulls on my hair, and the pain is excruciating but so good at the same time. She screams my name as she finishes, and I almost cum in my pants from the sweet sound of it. As she comes down from the high I kiss my way up to her face. Then I gently kiss her lips. I've never once been gentle with any woman or cared about someone as much as Angelina. But for her, I would go to hell if that meant she could experience heaven.

CHAPTER 19

Angelina

I stayed at Nico's again, and I love it here with him. At the same time, it feels like I'm in a whole other world, separate from reality. All of these lessons are new to me, and that should scare me, but if anything, it makes me fearless. I feel strong with and because of Nico.

My phone is going a-wall, so I finally take the time to check it. My father texted a thousand times, which was expected. I ignore all of them. Maybe one day I'll forgive him, but my blood is still boiling right now. My friends sent me so many texts that I legitimately cannot even read all of them. I decide to do a group FaceTime rather than read a book's worth of messages. Of course, they answer immediately.

"Angelina Vittori!" Gia yells.

"Where the fuck have you been?! You've been MIA for so long!" Rosie continues.

"Are you even alive, or is this some kind of recording? With today's technology, you never know," Gia rambles.

They go on and on for what feels like hours. I cut them both off before they ran out of breath.

"Calm your tits. Yes, I'm still alive and doing just fine. Better than fine. I have so much to tell you, but I can't do it over the phone. Next time I see you, I promise I'll spill."

"Ugh, you're going to make us wait. At least tell us what you've been doing these past few days!" Gia says.

I can't think of how to answer that question. I can't tell them about the mafia over the phone, and I'm not even sure I want to tell them anything. It's a dangerous job, and involving them could have consequences.

I tell them the truth but leave out certain details. "Nico has been helping me get back on my feet. It's been hard since my father sheltered me. After I left home, I didn't know where to live, where to go, or what to do with myself. I can't live in a hotel forever, nor can I be jobless. I've been staying with him the past few days, and he's helped me get my life back together piece by piece."

"Okay, if that's what's going on over there, then take all the time you need. I'm so happy for you, babe," Gia says.

"Just make sure he's not an ax murderer, please," Rosie adds.

"I miss you both so much, but I have to stay with Nico for a little longer. We have unfinished business to take care of," I say.

"We miss you too, but we can wait. After all, we used to go months without seeing you thanks to your piece of shit dad," Rosie says.

"Love you both," I say.

"Love you more," they reply in unison.

I hang up the phone and roll over to Nico. He's been awake the whole time, but I don't mind him listening to our conversation. So far, I have somehow ended up sleeping in his bed every night. I have a feeling even if I tried to sleep elsewhere, he would carry me to his room over his shoulder.

He brushes a piece of hair out of my face and says, "You can see your friends, you know. I want you all to myself, but I'm willing to share."

I smile. "Not yet. I miss them, but our training is my priority right now. I finally feel like I have a purpose."

"You never felt like you did before?" he asks.

"No. Not under my father's roof. I couldn't be myself, go anywhere, or do anything. There's no way I could have found my purpose as a rotting vegetable," I say.

His finger tenderly traces the line of my cheekbone and jaw. It's such a sweet gesture, I can't help but lean into his touch.

"I would never keep you from anything; I hope you know that," he says as if I didn't already know that.

An easy smile plays on my lips. "Of course I do. So, are you going to keep your word and teach me lesson six? After all, I wouldn't want you holding me back."

A mischievous grin overtakes his features, challenge accepted.

"Get dressed and meet me in the basement," he orders.

Nico leaves, so I change into my training suit once again. As I'm changing into it, the smell of fresh linen hits my nostrils, and I realize he washed it for me. Thank God, because I was sweating through it during last night's physical lesson. As usual, I throw my curls up into a ponytail and apply my lipstick. Maybe one day I'll try a color other than red, but that would feel like an act of betrayal. Red is my color.

Even though I've dressed the same for training these past few days, Nico still looks at me like I'm a goddess.

His eyes slowly roam from my head to my toes. I watch closely as his tongue glides across his teeth, and his eyes turn an even darker shade. Honestly, I can't tell whether he wants to fuck me or kill me. I love that about him. The sensual versus ruthless is what drew me to him in the first place.

He breaks eye contact and refocuses on why we're here in the first place. It's crazy how much I've learned from our lessons and grown as a woman in such a short amount of time. Nico has made me feel powerful and in complete control of my life. He is the reason I'm in this position, and I couldn't do it without him, but at the same time, I recognize that I am this woman because of me as well. Without the confidence I've felt, I couldn't do this. That was all me, and I'm so proud.

He points to the wall of guns to the right. Considering he has an entire inventory of guns I figured learning to shoot was a lesson. I've been waiting for this and hoping he'd teach me to use one.

"Lesson six, how to shoot a gun. Choose," he orders.

I look up at the wall. There are machine guns, pistols, shotguns, and so much more. I am familiar with most gun types, but only some of them. Just because I know the types, though, doesn't mean I know how to shoot one. Being stuck in my house all day, for every day of my life, did many favors for me research-wise. I'm pretty sure I know everything there is to know, just not the itty-bitty details of it all. It can be hard to educate yourself on these things without having it in front of you and basing it all on visuals.

A pistol catches my eye. It's small enough to put in my purse or strap to my thigh. I grab it from the wall and examine it. It's not too heavy and seems simple enough to learn.

"What's this one?" I ask.

"Black snub nose .38 special," he answers.

"I think I like it. I choose this," I say.

"That's one of my favorites. It's quick, effective, and sneaky," he says.

I follow him over to the paper targets he has set up. They're shaped like a person from the waist up. Right as I'm about to raise the gun and attempt a shot, Nico stops me. He's behind me, and I can feel his body inches from mine, with his lips next to my ear. He lowers my forearms so that I'm no longer holding the gun upright.

He speaks up. "Baby, you got to be patient. That could have gone very wrong, depending on the gun you're using. Some guns have a strong kickback. Knowledge is power, Angelina. Use that to your advantage. Never rely on a weapon for power. Rely, on this." He points to my head, and I nod in understanding.

"Every gun is different. I'll teach you how to use every single one on that wall if that's what you want. For now, focus on this one. It's yours," he says.

Most of our lessons consist of me acting and Nico talking. I take in every single word he says, and he takes in my every movement, watching for any mistakes. It works for us, and it's how I learn not only the best but the fastest in a short time. Every day that goes by is another day my father is partnered with Nico, and I need to replace him before he notices what we're doing.

"That gun carries five rounds. It does not have a hammer or safety, so it will immediately shoot when you pull the trigger. It may be small, but it can do plenty of damage," he says.

I smile. "Ooo stealthy and deadly. I like that."

"Reminds me of you," he whispers under his breath.

He turns me back around towards the target, puts one hand on my waist, and his other hand gives me the gun. He straightens my arms, places my finger over the trigger, and moves my other hand to the handle of the gun.

"Look through here to shoot. Those are the iron sights, and they'll help you aim. Line it up, and you'll hit your target exactly where you want to."

"Go for the head, chest, or gut to finish the job. If you just want to injure them, aim for their shoulder, arm, or leg. Most importantly, never point at anything you don't intend to shoot," he tells me.

I turn my head, and he's closer than I thought. My eyes meet his, and I hold them.

He nods. "Shoot whenever you're ready."

I turn my head back, raise the gun, and fix my stance. I straighten my arms, place my hands where he showed me, and look through the sights. I take a deep breath, stop my hands from shaking, and shoot.

When I lower my gun to see where it hit, I smile to myself—right in the center of the chest.

"Good. Now, do it again but faster. You won't have time to perfect your stance or aim when you need to use the gun. I'll give you three seconds to shoot this time, and if you're late," he leans in so his lips brush the delicate skin just under my ear, "You'll be punished for every extra second that passes."

I swallow and nod my head. Here's the thing about Nicolai, when he says something he means it. As much as I love the pain he inflicts on me, I'm determined to pass this lesson.

I raise the gun, and he whispers in my ear. Usually, the feel of his lips on my ear would make me shiver, but I don't think about his lips. I think about the gun in my hand and the target in front of me.

"Three," he counts down.

I straighten my arms, quickly fix my footing, and place my hands where I want them. I zone in on the target, never blinking or moving my eyes even in the slightest.

"Two," he says.

I shoot before he can say one.

My heart is racing, and my breathing is shallow. I look at the hole in the shoulder of the target. Not bad, but it wouldn't have killed them.

"We can work on that. After some more practice, your aim will be deadly," he says.

We shoot a few more rounds until both he and I are satisfied with my aim, stance, and knowledge of not only my gun but also a few others.

"Lesson six complete. You make it all look so easy, and I expected nothing less from you," he says.

He kisses my forehead, and my heart gushes every time he does that. It's such a tender act by such a ruthless man.

I whine, "I don't want to be done for the day."

I put my hands on his chest, bat my eyelashes, and pout my lips, trying my best to be convincing.

"Teach me more. Pretty please with a cherry on top."

"Anything for you, mio angelo. The next lesson isn't in my basement. Find something to wear at my club and change into that," he orders.

He slaps my ass as I run upstairs to change. I rifle through my bag full of clothes. I don't have many dress options, so I think of something else instead. I put on a black leather skirt and Nico's white button-up. I tuck half of it in to make it less baggy and more cute, leaving a few top buttons open to reveal some cleavage. Thankfully, the material of Nico's shirt is thick, so you can't see my black lacy bra through the white. I take my hair out of the ponytail and brush it out. My curls from last night died down after our lesson, and now my hair is back to its natural straight element. I throw on some mascara, reapply my red lipstick, and smother some vanilla lotion onto my legs. I look in the mirror, proud of this look. It's got a badass, hot receptionist vibe to it. It's the opposite of how I was forced to dress growing up, and I love it. I grab my new Saint Laurent heels and make my way down the stairs.

When he speaks, his voice sounds strained, as if he's struggling to breathe. "Holy Fuck."

The way Nico looks at me makes my knees go weak, and my legs throb. He's wearing black pants and a grey button-up. He exudes masculinity, and I eat him up. He smells like aftershave and expensive cologne, and it's all I want to breathe in for the rest of my life.

"Hope you don't mind me borrowing your shirt," I tell him.

"It looks way better on you. I love seeing you wearing my clothes, but I must admit I love seeing you without clothes more," he says mischievously.

He opens a door that leads to the garage, and my feet stop moving.

"Are these all yours?"

There are nearly five luxurious cars in here. One is the black Lamborghini I drove. I look around and see a red McLaren, a white Koenigsegg, a black Bugatti, and a grey Range Rover. These cars cost millions of dollars. I couldn't afford one of them, let alone five.

"Yours and mine. Pick one for today," he orders.

I walk around all of them and examine the outside and inside. They're sparkly clean and look brand new. I've noticed Nico is good at caring for things he cares about.

"How about the McLaren? Red's my favorite color," I say.

He looks at my lips as he speaks. "Mine too."

We arrive at Nico's club, and he has some work to catch up on as soon as we get there. I don't mind waiting in his office though; it's cozy in here. There is a dark marble desk against the wall and a black leather couch on the other side of the room.

Shelves fill the room, but they're empty, aside from some paperwork and decor. A mini fridge sits in the corner, and I open it to find champagne. I grab the bottle and a flute sitting nearby and fill it to the rim. I end up drinking half of the bottle by the time Nico gets back to the office an hour or so later. He comes in and locks the door behind him. I lean my ass against the front of his desk, take a sip of the champagne, and lick my lips, savoring the delicious flavor. It tastes expensive and has a lively acidity to it. Nico approaches me like a predator about to eat his prey, and I might just let him. He takes my glass out of my hands.

"How much have you had to drink Angelina?"

"Still on my first glass," I lie.

"Mm. You're getting better at lying, but not to me," he says.

Nico's knuckles lightly graze my neck and then move lower toward the buttons of my top. He starts to undo the buttons and I don't even care about the lesson anymore or why we came here. I'd rather be alone with him than anywhere else.

His voice is deep and sexy as he speaks. "Sit your pretty little ass up on my desk."

I do what he says. I'd do anything for him when he looks at me the way he is right now.

He steps in between my legs, forcing them apart, making my skirt raise to my thighs. He takes the glass from my hand and tilts the champagne glass down. As the liquid spills onto my chest, Nico leans over me and licks the wet trail it left behind. I tilt my head back, grab a fistful of his hair, and wrap my legs around his waist. The cold liquid mixed with his warm tongue sends me spiraling.

He comes face to face with me and claims my mouth. His hands go into my shirt and grip my hips roughly as his tongue explores my mouth. He pulls his mouth off mine, grabs my chin, and looks into my eyes.

"The next lesson isn't going to be easy, Angelina. You need to feel powerful and show it. Don't let them get to you because you're a woman in a crowd full of men. Understood?"

"Yes," I moan.

"Good."

He gets on his knees and looks up at me. "I get on my knees for no one. I submit to no one. I show weakness to no one. But for you, angel? You get all of me. You fucking own me. I bow to you and only you."

I've never seen Nico as vulnerable as he is now. What I love most about him is how he does not hold me back; he pushes me forward. He doesn't want the weak, innocent version of myself everyone expects me to be. He wants the cutthroat, resilient side of me. The dark parts I keep hidden. Those parts have always been a part of me, but they were never welcome and never came out. Without Nico, I'd still be an innocent little angel with hollow insides and zero purpose in life. Now, I am the truest version of myself because of him, with power, authority, and purpose.

The feel of Nico's tongue sliding up my inner thigh sends me out of my trance. He bites my inner thigh, and it stings. That will leave a mark, without a doubt.

"Ow! What was that for?" I shout.

Something must be seriously wrong with me because I swear the bite turned me on more. I may yell at him for it, but that doesn't mean I don't want it.

"That was for lying to me," he says.

He lightly kisses the bite mark, and what was once a stinging pain is now an undeniable pleasure.

"I've wanted another taste of you ever since I had one. I'm a man starved and craved. If I don't get you right here, I will lose. My. Fucking. Mind," he says, and I can tell he means it.

His words ring true because he doesn't wait a second longer. He grips my hips and pulls me forward toward his face. His tongue thrusts inside of me and my eyes roll to the back of my head. I fist his hair, desperate for something to keep me grounded. Seeing Nico on his knees makes me feel powerful but not in complete control when he's the one making the moves. I want him to unravel because of me; I want him to beg, and I want to make the demands. Even though it's nearly impossible to resist his tongue, I pull on his hair so hard that he's forced to look up at me. I slowly raise my leg, drag my heel up his arm, and then push my heel against his chest, forcing him to back up.

I hop off the desk, grab his hand, and lead him to the other side toward his desk chair. He takes in every one of my movements, never once questioning my actions. *What a good boy.*

"Sit," I order.

Nico is not the type to take orders, but he obeys my demands.

I raise my skirt, sit on top of his lap, and un-do his button-up and tie. His fingers leave imprints on my ass as I grind against him.

"Fuck, baby," he hisses under his breath.

I free his raging cock, and slowly sit down on it. I move at the pace I want, and Nico lets me. He doesn't take away my control even in the slightest bit. Once I feel like I'm about to go over the edge I ride him fast and hard with a last command.

"You cum when I say so," I tell him.

"Making demands now, angel?"

I smirk. "Bet your sweet ass I am."

"Yes, ma'am," he says.

I continue riding him and watch him the whole time. I can tell when he's close, so a few times, I slow down just to remind him how in control I am.

"Baby, I love this side of you, but if you don't let me cum soon, I will flip you over and punish you for this fucking torture you're putting me through," he says.

I lean in so close to his ear that it leaves a red imprint on his cheek.

"Beg," I order.

His face is covered with shock by what I asked, but then a slow grin stretches across it. He looks proud of my audacity.

"You heard me. Beg."

"Per favore, mio angelo," he says with his smooth, sexy Italian accent.

I bounce on his cock at a pace that sends him wild, and I'm crying out his name at this point. He's cursing and bruising me all over with his grip to restrain himself from finishing without permission. I can see in his eyes how desperate he is for release.

"Such a good boy," I praise.

He growls at my words since they are not what he wants to hear. I don't want my poor baby to be suffering, so I give him what he wants, what he oh so desperately needs.

I whisper in his ear, "Cum for me, Nico."

As soon as the words leave my mouth he stands, picks me up, and throws my back on the desk with so much force I thought it would break. He scoots my ass to the edge and fucks me as he's standing. He's not polite about it, and neither is the way he's fucking. I won't admit it to him, but I love it when his feral side comes out to play.

"Nic—"

"Shut your pretty red mouth. You can take it."

His fucking is painful, rough, and full of need. I love it.

"God, you feel so good," he groans.

He pounds into me, and I'm certain that the desk has moved across the room at this point, and the whole club can hear us even over the music.

As soon as his hand cuts off my airways, my orgasm rushes through me. My head leans back over the other side of his desk, giving me an upside-down view of his office. My body remains getting fucked on the desk, and I ride out the rest of my orgasm as he fucks me harder, with more and more less air. He pulls out and explodes all over me. The button-up I'm wearing has almost fallen off of me, so thankfully, it doesn't get covered in our mess. At this point, we're both breathless and satisfied, forgetting why we came here in the first place.

We straighten ourselves up and fix Nico's trashed office. I look in the mirror and fix my lipstick, makeup, and tangled hair. By the time I'm finished, I look good as new.

"Ready for your next lesson?" he asks.

"Bring it on," I say.

"That's my girl. Take a seat. You have some learning to do before you run with the big guys."

As he approaches, I sit down in his desk chair. He comes around to the front of the desk and reaches across me to open a drawer. What he pulls out is not what I expected.

A deck of playing cards.

CHAPTER 20

Nicolai

Teaching Angelina how to play poker has intrigued me more than I'd like to admit. She listens to every word I say and etches it all into her brain. She's so eager to learn that it makes my dick twitch. I'd love to take her to my bedroom and see her eagerness to learn there. *Focus, Nico.* I explain the game to her once more to make sure she understands.

"All players are dealt two cards face down, followed by three community cards. Five community cards will eventually make their way face-up," I say.

I give her two cards and lay the others on the desk before us.

"To win, you must have the best poker hand using the hand you're dealt and the five community cards. Got it?" I ask.

"You don't have to repeat yourself. I got it the first time," she says with little patience.

She smirks, and I grin back at her as I lean in close.

"Watch the attitude, or I'll take you over my desk, and not kindly, angel," I warn her.

That shuts her up. To be honest, I don't mind her little attitude flares now and then. They're cute and sexy as hell, considering she's the only one with the audacity to talk back to me.

"So, what's the best poker hand?" she asks.

"A royal flush. They're hard to get, but possible. The order goes royal flush, straight flush, four-of-a-kind, full house, flush, straight, three-of-a-kind, two pair, pair, and high card. It's a lot to take in all at once, but after a few plays, you'll get the hang of it," I answer.

I explain all of the hands in the best way I can, but they're easiest to learn by playing rather than telling. I would know, considering that's how I learned as a kid. My parents tried explaining them to me, but then found out I got the hang of it by practicing. Teaching Angelina to play poker like my parents did for me hits a soft spot in my heart. I've never taught anyone before. I always kept it to myself, unwilling to tell anyone about my family. Poker was the one thing I shared with my parents, and it made them proud of me. It was our thing, but right now, I want nothing more than to share it with her.

"You'll get better the more games you play, but I can give you a few tips for now. First, never fold on the flop. But also, don't stick around hoping to get lucky on the river," I explain.

She nods.

"Next, always observe your opponents. Everyone has a tell if you can catch it. Which is why you need to keep your composure always. Do not sweat, show emotion, bounce your leg, or do anything of the sort. Just like a lie, it will give you away."

"Lastly, never cheat, or in other words, don't get caught. If you get caught up there, you get killed. It's a rule that's been enforced for years, and no one is shown mercy when it happens. Understood?" I ask.

"Yes," she says.

We start a game, just us two in my office. She's getting closer to being ready, but not quite yet. The men who play in the VIP lounge have been playing for years. But they're no experts considering I beat their ass every night and let them pity win on occasion.

I deal the cards out and look at my hand. She could beat it if she tries, but that all depends on her gameplay. I look at her over my hand. She is focused and doesn't once show an ounce of indecision. She looks up and catches me staring but doesn't smile or change her facial expression. She shows zero emotion, and damn, I am proud of her for it.

I win the game and the next two that follow. On the fourth game, she comes close to winning, and that's when I decide she's ready. If she can come close to beating me, of all people, she can beat the guys upstairs.

"Let's go," I order.

She stops walking. "Wait."

I turn around and see her remove another button on her top.

"Now is not a good time, angel," I tell her even though I don't want to refuse a round two.

"No, it's not for you. You have your advantages, and I have mine," she shrugs.

I shake my head. This woman. The last thing she should be doing is dangling a lollipop in front of their faces and then denying them a taste. But I'll be near, and I'll be damned if they even lick their lips.

She adjusts her bra and hair and then raises her skirt higher. Now that's not happening. I walk up to her and pull it down back where it was.

"Absolutely not," I say without room for debate.

She giggles, thinking her little stunt was funny. I smack her ass hard for it and then grab her hand, leading us toward the door.

Right before we enter the VIP lounge upstairs, I whisper in her ear, "Do not let them scare you. They are a bunch of pricks with giant egos. They all bark, no bite. You show them some real teeth in there, yeah?"

"I'm not scared. Not with you beside me," she says.

Pretty sure my heart just melted all over the fucking place. I open the door and place my hand on her back as she walks in. I'm going to make it clear that she belongs to me. She approaches the poker table like she owns the room. Head held high, face expressionless, and voice fearless. She sits down at the green, circular table, and I stand behind her. I want to watch her play the game, not compete against her in it.

"Deal her in," I say to the dealer.

All the men around look her way and smirk. I can read their thoughts. Some of them are assuming this game will be easy, and others are thinking of all the ways to fuck her. I stare at the men checking her out until they look my way. They stop gawking at her as soon as they catch me giving them the death glare. I will pop their eyeballs out of their sockets in seconds if they look at her again with lust.

I lean down before they start handing out cards. I won't be allowed to speak to her once the game starts, considering it'd look like I'm helping her. But the least I can do is help her out before the game begins. I whisper as quietly as I can, ensuring no one can eavesdrop on my secrets.

"The guy on the left crosses his ankles when he's bluffing. The one on the right cracks his neck when he has a bad hand. And the one across from you is the one you need to keep an eye on. He's the best here below me and is good at hiding his lies. If you watch him closely enough, you can see that he blinks when he gets a card he likes. Count his blinks to see how good of a hand he has. You got this, baby."

She turns her head and looks up at me. "Thank you, Nico."

I nod. I know she can do this.

The dealer hands out the cards, and I step back but remain close enough to peek at her hand. She immediately has a two-pair, but that's not a winnable hand in most cases. She looks to her left and catches the guy crossing his ankles. She looks ahead but doesn't lift her head much, not wanting to grab any attention. The guy across from her grabs a community card and blinks twice. She catches it. Then she hears the guy to her right crack his neck.

All that she is up against is the guy across from her and she knows it. She picks up one of the face-down cards, which doesn't help her hand whatsoever. The guy to her left folds. Then the guy across adds in two more chips. The next guy is an idiot and stays in the game even though his hand likely sucks. He is in so much gambling debt it will get him killed soon. Angelina contemplates her hand for a moment but eventually folds. It was the smart thing to do, or she would have lost a good amount of money.

She sits back as the two men reveal their hands. The guy across had a straight, and the one to the right had three-of-a-kind. Angelina shows the two pairs she had, but it wouldn't have been enough to beat a straight. She didn't lose, but she didn't necessarily win either. I expect her to back down after the game, but she doesn't.

"Deal me in again," she orders.

The same three guys stay in the game, but a fourth approaches the table. I didn't even see him enter the room. Rocco fucking Accardi. He still thinks we're business partners since we haven't replaced Enzo yet. I'm supposed to be taking time off right now so I'm hoping he doesn't call me out about being here.

"Deal me in," he says.

He sits right beside Angelina, too close for my liking.

Rocco is no poker king, but he's just about as good as the guy across from her. I can't help her since I don't know what his tells are, and the game has already begun.

Before they pick up their hands, Rocco leans into Angelina. Considering that's all I focus on, I can hear what he says and he's not exactly trying to whisper.

"Haven't seen your face here before. It's nice to have a fresh pair of pretty eyes in the room," he flirts.

My nostrils flare, and my expression clouds in anger. I seethe but do my best to remain calm. I can't cause a scene during a game, but if he so much as touches her, I will slice his throat from behind him in an instant.

She doesn't reply to his comment or even look his way. Seeing her so resilient to the presence of any man who isn't me brings me so much satisfaction. Call me cocky for it, clingy, possessive I don't care. *She's mine.*

I look over her shoulder, and she has a good hand— almost a full house. She doesn't fidget, make a face, or do anything to give her away. Even I wouldn't be able to tell what she has if I were playing against her. It's impressive.

She easily catches the other two fidgeting, and the one across blinks once. She turns her head slightly down and left toward Rocco, but not enough to make him notice her stare. She looks right where I do, at his foot jumping in the slightest. She noticed his tell without my help. She picks up a card, and it's exactly what she needs. She has a full house, and that's hard to beat. Rocco picks up another card and continues bouncing his foot. The guys diagonal and to the right of her both fold. The one across adds in three chips. All that's left is Angelina, the guy across, and Rocco. She adds four chips, upping his challenge.

Rocco adds in five, but we both know he doesn't have shit. He underestimates her, as does everyone else here.

Rocco laid his cards down and said, "Flush."

The guy across goes next with a grin. He thinks he will win, and reality is about to slap him in his smug face. He can't beat her full house.

"Full house." He surprises me.

Oh shit. Angelina is the last to go, but I have already seen her hand. They'll tie.

"Full house, aces high," she says confidently.

The men are all too stunned to speak, as am I. Where did she get those aces? Rocco just smiles at her like he's her proud boyfriend, and I am suddenly elated I won't be working with him much longer.

I walk up to Angelina and offer my hand to her. She takes it and stands.

With one final glance at the table, she says, "Good game, boys. Until next time."

Calling a room full of men boys is an insult to their masculinity, and she knows it. They don't scare her, and she just proved that. I am so proud of her right now that I don't even hide my emotions in this room. For the first time, I grin like a lovestruck fool in front of everyone.

As soon as we make it out the door, I push her against the wall, grab her and kiss the fuck out of her. I claim her as mine, and she melts into my touch.

"I am so fucking proud of you right now, baby. Just be careful. You might not always get so lucky in poker," I warn her.

"I always have an ace up my sleeve," she says with a wink.

So that's how she won. My conniving, sneaky little angel.

"Lesson seven, check!" she says happily.

I kiss her neck and cheek all over her face, then back to those delicious red lips.

"How many more, Nico?" she whines and pouts, and oh god, the things I would do to see her make that face on her knees begging for me.

"Just one, baby, just one."

The last lesson is the hardest and I'm really worried about it. It's the most important test, and if she can't pass it, I'm not sure she can be part of my world or with me at all. It's a part of who I am and what I do. If she does pass it, I'd marry her in a heartbeat, knowing she's my fucking soulmate.

I lead her to the club's basement but stop before opening the door. I take a deep breath.

"Angelina, if you can't do this lesson, tell me, okay? We can leave immediately," I say, my voice full of caution.

"Yeah, okay," she says like I'm being dramatic.

She sees the worry in my eyes.

"Nico, whatever it is, I can handle it."

I nod, deciding to trust her words. This could be the moment I lose her forever or find out she's mine forever.

I open the door and go in first. She follows behind. When I step out of her vision, I hear her suck in a breath of air.

There's a man tied to a chair in the middle of the basement. He's covered in blood because I told my employees to roughen him up a bit but leave him alive for us.

She sees the guy and then immediately looks back at me.

"Nico?" Her voice is full of question, but confusion is better than anger, hurt, or fear.

I can already see her thoughts spiraling and her internal self freaking out. I turn her around so she can't see him, only me.

"That man sitting right there? He raped and impregnated his daughter. Then he killed her and got away with it," I say.

I made sure to choose someone who deserved this fate.

I go on. "Men like him shouldn't live. They don't deserve mercy. He deserves everything coming to him."

She starts her words off slowly. "Okay. I agree. But what am I doing here?"

"Last lesson: kill him," I order.

She just stands there in shock and then looks at him. I start to wonder if this is a mistake.

"How old?" she asks.

"He's forty-eight," I answer.

"No. The daughter."

I close my eyes and take a breather to calm myself.

"Fourteen."

Her face turns into a mask of rage, and her eyes well up with tears, but she dries her eyes before they can fall. I can tell she's contemplating what to do. She looks up and meets my eyes.

"Do you trust me?" she asks.

"Always, baby. Always."

"Good. Then leave him to me, and don't interrupt unless I say so," she orders.

Her eyes turn dark and insolent. It's like watching an angel turn into a devil.

She turns around and walks toward the man. I stand back, arms crossed, and watch her. This lesson is important, and I can't baby her, no matter how badly I want to. I leave this man's death completely in her hands.

As she approaches him, she unbuttons her top, revealing the top of her cleavage and lacy bra. She raises her skirt, which angers me, but I don't interfere. I don't understand why she's teasing him, but I stand still and obey her previous orders.

She walks up to him, and he looks her up and down. He can't deny being attracted to her; no one can. She removes the tape covering his mouth, and he yells. He can scream all he wants, but this basement is completely soundproof. She pushes her finger against his mouth.

Her voice comes out kind and sweet. "Shh. I'm not going to hurt you. I just came to have a little fun."

He quiets his screams and eyes her carefully. He's cautious of her presence but turned on based on the bulge in his pants. I am so jealous of Angelina right now because I would love to kill him slowly. She sits on his lap, and my fingernails dig into my fists so hard I feel blood drip. She starts to move on him, and I'm very close to interrupting this stunt she's pulling right in front of me. What the fuck is she thinking?

"Do you like that?" she asks.

His hands and feet are tied, so he can't touch her, but I can see how badly he wants her. Badly enough that I can tell he'd take her without consent.

"You are so hot," he says. His nasty, old voice reached over to where I was standing.

"Yeah? Is that what you told your daughter?" she asks, changing her tone.

"What the fuck! Get off me, you sick bitch," he shouts and squirms.

She laughs. It's not her usual light, pretty laugh, though. No, this one is full of viciousness, and it's terrifying.

"I'm the sick bitch here? Really? What was her name?" She asks.

"Get off of me!" he yells louder.

She reaches behind her, untucks her shirt, and grabs a knife out of the back of her skirt. I didn't even know she had that with her. *Impressive*.

She points the knife at his pants, right where his hard-on is.

"What. Was. Her. Name," she orders.

He gives in. "Fuck. Fuck! Okay. Ava. Her name was Ava."

She spits in his face, then gets off his lap. She buttons her shirt back up and pulls her skirt back down. She starts circling him while examining her knife.

"Did you rape her? Did you rape your daughter?" she asks.

When he doesn't answer, she stops circling and points the knife so it's lightly touching his pants.

"Answer me!" she yells.

He breaks out in sobs. It's quite sad, but I would never pity scum like him.

"Yes, I raped her. I had to kill her; I had no choice! You understand, right? She couldn't have my child. I would go to jail!" he shouts as if she will sympathize with him.

She scrapes the knife down his face lightly. "Oh, honey. Jail would be heaven compared to my wrath."

She raises it and stabs him in the crotch, which I did not expect. He cries in pain.

"What the fuck! You said you wouldn't hurt me!" he screams.

He bends over as much as he can with his hands tied and throws up on the floor and all over himself. Then he starts gagging from the pain of his dick getting stabbed.

"Oh, you've got a hell of a lot more where that came from."

She slowly drags the knife up his leg to his chest, deep enough to leave a trail of blood in its wake. She leans in and looks into his eyes.

"No one will remember you, and I don't have to worry about you going to hell after this life. You're already there," she says.

God damn.

She takes her time with him, and I don't mind waiting. I watch every second. She scalps him, slaps him, and, worst of it all, she pops both his eyes out with her knife. I've never heard someone cry in so much pain, and I realize how easy I've been to my past captives. By the time she's finished, he's barely alive. He's panting and crying for help. Asking God for mercy.

"All you can see is darkness. That's all you'll ever see. God will not save you. He didn't save Ava, so why would he save you? But the difference between you and her? She will be remembered by me, the woman who brought her justice," she says firmly.

As the words leave her mouth, she slices his jugular, leaving him to bleed out all over the floor.

I am stuck in my spot, still standing, completely entranced by her. She made him suffer worse than I could have even tried. Emotionally and physically. Angelina Vittori has the face of an angel and the mind of a killer.

At this moment, I realize I'm deeply in love with Angelina Vittori. She was made for me. And I'll be damned if I don't spend eternity with her as my partner in crime.

CHAPTER 21

Angelina

I completely blacked out the moment Nico told me what he did to that poor girl. I have never killed someone before or even considered it, but after he admitted to it, there was no way I was letting him walk the streets and hurt another girl. Nico orders his employees to clean up my mess and the body, and they get rid of it within minutes.

Nico's white button-up that I'm wearing is covered in blood. There's no way the stains will come out. My hands are dripping in it, and the floor is slippery because of the mess I made. But none of this bothers Nico when he comes up and kisses me. He kisses me with delicacy and tenderness. It's a type of kiss I haven't experienced with him before. Typically, they're full of need and desperation, but it's pure sweet intent right now. It's what I needed.

"Baby, I have no words for what that was," he says.

He gently laughs and shakes his head.

He goes on. "I am enthralled by you. You're beauty, strength, every single part of you."

He leans down, and his forehead meets mine, and his hands hold both sides of my face.

"I am so foolishly in love with you, mio angelo," he says, catching me off guard.

"It took a murder for you to figure that out?!" I ask.

I slap him on his chest lightly and crack a laugh. I am in love with Nicolai Leone. He gets me like no one else. He knows what I need even when I don't know it myself. He has brought out parts of me I kept hidden, and I am a better woman because of it.

I walk up to him, grab his tie, and pull him to me. "Then that makes two fools because I am in love with you Nico."

I kiss him with more need than the last kiss. I shove my tongue in his throat, and he groans. The blood all over me is, without a doubt, covering him, but I must admit, we look good in red.

"On your knees, angel," he orders.

I hold his eyes as I drop to my knees. The hard concrete is digging into my knees and is colder than ice, but I don't care.

"Did you think I would let you grind on that man and not punish you for it? I almost stepped in to kill him myself for even looking at you that way. No one gets to see you the way I do. Got that?" He asks, even though there's only one right answer.

"I had to prove he did it, and the only way was for me to see for myself," I explain.

He grabs my jaw and makes me look up at him.

"The only thing that should be coming out of your mouth is 'Yes, Nico'."

"Yes, Nico," I say.

"Open wide, baby."

I open and stick my tongue out, eager for him.

"Greedy little thing," he says.

He unzips his pants and takes his hard-on out. It leaks with pre-cum, and I go to lick it off, but before I can, Nico pulls my head back by my hair.

"Did I give you permission?"

"Since when do I need permission?" I know I shouldn't be giving him attitude right now, but poking the bear is just too much fun.

"Since I say so. Tell me, angel, does God know what you do with that mouth of yours? With that cunt? I'd bet you if he did, he'd have no problem with you going straight to hell with me," he says.

He puts a finger on my chin and lifts my head. "Would you go to hell with me?"

"Yes, Nico," I say and mean it.

"Good answer. Now suck," he orders.

I take my time at first, wanting to tease him to the edge of sanity. I lick from his shaft to the tip. Repeatedly. Driving him mad on purpose.

"If you can't suck me like you mean it, I'll make you," he warns.

I love a good challenge. I hold his eyes and slowly take my mouth out with a pop, then kiss his tip, leaving a red lip imprint where my lips were.

"You want to play dirty? I'll play dirty," he says with a cruel tone.

He grabs the back of my head and shoves his dick in my mouth. I moan, loving the feral side of him. He shoves back farther and farther, almost like he's trying to make me choke. I won't let him win this one, though, so grab the back of his thighs and push him forward, taking him as deep as he can go. My eyes water and mascara runs down my face, but I won't give in.

"Such a good girl, but a filthy mouth indeed."

I raise my hands to his ass and deepen my fingernails into his skin, leaving scratches in its trail.

"Touch yourself," he orders.

I look up at him with hesitation in my eyes.

"I wasn't asking."

I move my hand down my body and then up my skirt, all while holding his dick in my mouth with the other.

I feel myself dripping for him, which doesn't surprise me. His dirty words, desperate cock, and pure lust in his eyes are enough to soak any woman through their panties.

I quicken my pace with my fingers as I do with my mouth.

He pulls his dick out of my mouth, and I'm just left here on my knees, touching myself.

"I want to see all of you while I cover you in my cum," he says breathlessly.

I remove my hand, but Nico shakes his head, warning me not to do that.

"I didn't tell you to stop," he warns.

I don't listen, even though I probably should. I move my hands to my button-up and rip it open before I grip my breasts and play with my tits for him.

"Fucking bellissima," he groans.

I keep one hand playing with my tits and bring the other back under my skirt. My pussy is begging for release.

Nico approaches me, grips my neck, and forces me to look into his eyes.

"You finish when I do."

"Yes, Nico," I moan.

I match his pace and watch him, never pulling my eyes away.

"Fuck, baby."

I scream his name as I ride out my orgasm. Not a second longer, his cum shoots out on my neck, dripping down to my breasts. I'm a complete mess covered in a stranger's blood, Nico's cum, and my arousal.

"You've never looked more beautiful than you do now. You paint such a pretty picture, mio angelo," he says.

Luckily, Nico has spare clothes here, so I can leave the club without looking like a scene from Carrie mixed with Sex in the City.

He brushes my hair as I button up a new top, and the sweet gesture makes my heart gush. Nico has dark parts of him that he makes sure everyone sees, but in private, he saves the light parts for me. I love both sides of him, just as he does me.

As were on our way home I realized I could use some of the stuff I left at the hotel. I'd prefer to not use men's hair wash any longer.

"Can we stop at the hotel? I'd like to grab a few more of my things," I ask.

Nico slows the car down and pulls off the side of the road.

"Um, the hotel is that way," I tell him as I point in the other direction.

He looks at me. "I know where it is. We can stop at the hotel but not for a few things—for all your things. You're moving in with me."

"Are you asking or telling me?"

"Either way, I'm not taking no for an answer," he says.

"Bossy much?"

"Keep up this attitude, and I'll show you bossy," he warns.

I sigh, even though I'm loving this. "Fine. I'll move in with you against my own will."

I joke with him, but secretly, I'm all giddy inside. I love waking up next to Nico or, in some cases, with him between my legs in the morning. Everything with him feels so natural, and I'd love nothing more than to live together. We're moving faster than normal, but time isn't a factor when you're with the right person. Nico lost his parents when he was young, so I'm sure he doesn't take things for granted, and neither do I. I am finally away from my father. I lost eighteen years of my life to him; I'm not going to lose anymore by taking things for granted or being patient about our relationship.

I reach across the console and kiss Nico on the cheek. A gentle smile splays across his lips as he pulls back on the road.

We made it to the hotel a few minutes later.

"You can stay. It'll only be a minute or two. I don't have that much stuff," I say.

"Okay. But any longer, and I'm coming up there. Call me if you need me. I'll be here."

I went up to my room and packed up my things: my hair care products, perfume, a few clothes I left behind, and makeup. All I brought was two duffel bags full, so I left with one since my other was already at the house—*our house.*

When Nico sees me walking out of the hotel, he comes up to me and takes my bag out of my hands. He throws it over his shoulder as we walk to his car.

"I called your father while you were in there. I set up a meeting with him for tomorrow morning. Are you ready?"

"Yeah. After all, I didn't go through all those lessons for nothing. I want to be your partner, not him. He lost that privilege the moment he lied to you," I say.

"No. He lost that privilege the moment he laid his hands on my woman."

CHAPTER 22

Nicolai

When I called Enzo yesterday, he sounded angry and impatient. Probably because I have been so distracted and distant lately. I'm prepared for any outcome of this meeting. He's already pissed off, and I can say with certainty that replacing him as my partner will infuriate him, especially doing so with the daughter he's kept sheltered for so long. That's not going to stop me from doing it, though. I'd do anything for that girl, and she's earned this position.

I put on a black suit and red tie, my new favorite combination. Angelina wears the short black dress she wore the night I first laid eyes on her. It might be my favorite, but then again, I say that about everything she wears.

"I'm not so sure your father will like that, but I sure as hell do," I say.

I walk up to her and kiss her deeply. I seriously will never get enough of this girl. I grab a handful of her ass and groan into her mouth. As much as I'd love to take her as mine, being late for this meeting is not a good idea. No need to piss the man off more than he already is.

"I'm almost ready. I have to grab a few more things first. Do you have anything with you?" I ask her.

She lifts her leg onto a nearby chair and pushes her dress up. That's when I see the three knives strapped onto her thigh.

I smile. "That's my girl."

I go down to the basement and grab a gun off the wall. Angelina's choice, the black snub nose .38 special. I tuck it into my pants and hide it with my suit jacket. I pray I won't need to use it, but I need a way to protect Angelina if we get into a situation. I hate her bastard of a father for how he treated her, and I would have killed him by now for hitting her if I thought she could forgive me for it. I don't know if she could, and I would never do anything that could make me lose her. Now, if Enzo pulls any shit tonight with her around, that's a whole other scenario that would likely end in bloodshed. I won't kill her father unless he gives me no choice. I'd rather her hate me than be dead.

We pull up to Angelina's childhood house. I'd say home, but that's not what this is. I park in his driveway and look over at her. She's eerily calm.

"Say when, angel," I tell her.

"Go ahead. I know the plan."

I step out and head to the front door, while she remains behind. She will come inside when I message her. There is no need to overwhelm Enzo all at once. He has no idea we even know each other, let alone work together. I knock and hear heavy footsteps shortly after. Angelina leans down in the car so he doesn't see her out front.

Enzo opens the door. "Nicolai, it's about damn time you got out of vaycay mode. Come on in."

His joking indicates he's way calmer and more collected than he was on the phone last night. His mood always does this, though. One moment he's an asshole, and the next a sucker-up. It's one thing that always pissed me off about our partnership. You never knew what would tick him off, and it was a dangerous game to be around him all these years. He would do things I didn't agree with just because someone spilled a drink on him or looked at him the wrong way.

"Why did you want to meet, son? The club seems to be doing just fine, and I've been handling business while you were gone."

Yet another thing ticked me off in our partnership. He always called me "son" and claimed he raised me. He is nothing like my father and has no right to call me that nickname. He may have helped me make my way up to mafia boss, but that does not mean he raised me—not even in the slightest.

I text Angelina and tell her to come in quietly. I see her sneak in behind Enzo and hide behind a wall. She will know when to step in.

"That's great, but that's not why I'm here. I have news," I say.

"Alright, get on with it," he says impatiently.

I put my hands in my pocket to resist the itch to grab my gun behind my back and protect her from him. I've never been scared of Enzo. Even when he was old and powerful while I was a helpless little boy, he didn't scare me. Right now, though, I'm terrified of him around Angelina and how he will react. He's either going to take this bad or very bad.

"I no longer need your partnership," I admit.

He just stares at me like he didn't hear me.

"Pardon?" he asks.

"I quit."

"You can't quit; I made you. You have everything because of me!" he yells.

He closes his eyes, takes a deep breath, and calms down. This time, when he speaks, his voice is normal volume. "You know what. I don't need you. Do whatever you want, Nicolai, but you will not survive alone."

"Oh, I won't be. I have a new partner," I tell him.

I wink at her from where she is peeking around a corner, signaling her to come out.

When she walks in, everything feels like it's in slow motion. She straightens her posture, sways her hips as she walks, and brushes her hair over her shoulder. She doesn't look at her father's shocked face until she's standing beside me with my arm around her hip. She's so badass and beautiful and *mine*. She looks to her father, and her confidence never falters.

"Father," she greets him.

"What the fuck is going on here?" Enzo asks.

"Enzo, meet my new partner." I look at Angelina.

He bends over on his knees and laughs hysterically. Not the reaction I was expecting, and frankly, it pisses me off.

"No part of this is funny, and you better hope you're not laughing at her," I warn.

"You're joking, right? She is as fragile as a baby. She doesn't know shit. She will fail you at the first opportunity," he says.

"Watch your fucking mouth," I snarl.

Angelina places a hand on my chest before I do something I regret. She knows that calms me down. I nod, reassuring her that I'm alright.

Yet I'm not the one who needs calming because what she does next is not something I ever saw coming, or I would have stopped it.

The black snub nose tucked in the back of my pants is now in her hands and pointed at her father.

"You don't control me anymore and won't speak about me that way. Got it?"

"Wow. So that's what I get for raising you. I gave you a roof to live under, a car, food, and for what? To have a gun pointed at me?"

Angelina walks closer to him with the gun still in her hand. "See, that's where you're wrong. You didn't give me a life;

you took it. My friends, personality, socials, school, all of it. I lost eighteen years to you because of your control. I was nothing more to you than a pup on a tight leash, and I am done," she says.

She goes on, "Maybe one day I will be more forgiving, but right now I feel nothing for you. I am Nico's partner and you will let it be. You will grow a fucking pair and get over it."

Holy hell. *I am so proud of her.*

"Nicolai, are you really on her side? I raised you, too. You're like a son to me. Does that mean nothing?" he asks, truly hurt and shocked.

I almost feel bad for the prick. *Almost.*

"I appreciate what you did for me, but you did not make me the man I am today. My parents did. They taught me everything I know. I am grateful for the opportunities you gave me, but no matter who or what helped me, I would have gotten there regardless," I say.

Angelina lowers the gun, turns, and walks out. She's said all she needs to. I follow behind, and when I take one last glance at Enzo, his face is pure anger, but I don't care. As she said, he can grow the fuck up.

When I get in the car, I see Angelina's mask falter. Her eyes start to water, so I lean across and wipe her tears before they fall.

"Don't cry for him, baby. He doesn't deserve your tears," I say.

Her voice comes out wobbly and sad. "I know, but what kind of a father says that about their kid?"

The crack in her voice punches me in the gut.

"He doesn't deserve to be a father, let alone yours. Don't listen to his words; they're not true, and we both know it. You're one of the smartest people I know, and you're capable of doing anything you put your mind to. You did great and I'm so proud of you," I tell her.

She nods and focuses on her breathing. I kiss her lightly and feel her relax. Her breathing calms, and her eyes dry.

"I'm sorry for taking your gun. I lost it when he talked shit in front of me about me. I may have allowed that in the past, but things have changed. I've changed," she says.

"Don't ever apologize to me. You could've put a bullet through his head, and I wouldn't care. I trust you wholeheartedly. I was just worried about how he would react. Thankfully he didn't pull out a gun of his own," I say.

"Yeah. I think the meeting went well. Except for the shit that came out of his mouth," she replies.

"It did go well. I know Enzo; he handled it better than I expected."

"Take me home, Nico."

CHAPTER 23

Angelina

A night out after that shit show is exactly what I need. My father handled it exactly as I expected, with his hurtful words and pissed-off glares. I'm just glad it didn't end in bloodshed.

I text my friends in our group chat, hoping they'll meet up with me soon. I always have such a fun time with them, and it's time they finally meet Nico.

FBGM Group Chat

Angelina: I miss you guys. Want to meet at *La Citta del Peccato* in an hour or so? I could use a drink.

Gia: Hell, yes, girl. I'll be there.

Rosanna: Me too. Gia, I'll drive us; we both know you like to get tipsy. Angelina, do you want a ride?

Angelina: Nico will drive me. Thanks though. I'm so excited! It's been too long since we've had a girls' night. I'm dragging Nico along so you can finally meet him. Plus, I could use a lookout while I'm drinking! Just think of him as one of the girls for the night! (Pls don't tell him I said that)

Rosanna: Can he look out for Gia, too? She can be a handful.

Gia: Hey! Wait, that's kind of true. OMG, remember that time I got so drunk you guys couldn't find me, and I was outside asleep next to a homeless guy? That was SO funny.

Rosanna: Dear lord, help me.

Angelina: I hate being hungover, but I'll get plastered any day with my girls. Let's get fucked up! You too, Rosie!

Gia: Period, sis!

Rosanna: Lmao. See you two later. Gia be ready in forty minutes.

Gia: Easy Peasy!

Angelina: Love you!

Gia and Rosanna: Love you more!

My face is lit up in a huge smile as I'm texting. I miss them more than life. They would drop everything they were doing just to see me, and I'd do the same for them. Nico comes up behind me as I sit on the couch, leaning down to kiss my cheek.

"Are they in?" he asks.

"Oh, they're always in for a good time," I say.

"I'm glad you'll get to see them. You deserve a fun night out," he says sweetly.

"Thank you, Nico. You're so good to me," I say.

"I'll never be anything less. You deserve the best, mio angelo." Every time he calls me that, it flows off his tongue so well. The accent, the way his voice deepens, and his pupils darken. Goosebumps erupt all over my skin every. Single. Time.

I only have an hour to get ready, surprisingly not much compared to what I'm used to. I throw my hair in a classy low bun and put some makeup on my face, including red lipstick. I wear a black dress, similar to my other black one but different in style. This one has long, sheer sleeves and a tight skirt that constantly rides up my legs. I put on the black Saint Laurent heels Nico bought me, a pair of gold earrings, and a necklace I recently bought. I ordered it online with my money so Nico wouldn't notice. I was barely able to hide the package when it arrived. I hook it on, look in the mirror, and walk downstairs, where he awaits me.

He always looks at me like I'm the prettiest woman in the room. His face lights up, eyes darken, and he licks his lips like I'm his next meal. I'll never get tired of him looking at me this way.

I walk up to him close enough that our lips almost touch, and his eyes trail down to the necklace I'm wearing. He lightly picks it up with his fingers and examines it.

"Is this for me, angel?" he asks, with hope in his expression.

"Duh. N for Nicolai. Right around my neck so people know who I belong to," I tell him.

He pulls on the necklace, not hard enough to break it, but enough to make me lean into him. He puts his other hand in my hair and kisses me sweetly like he's thanking me. When I saw this necklace online, I knew I had to order it, not only for me but for him. I want people to know I'm his, and I'm sure he does too. We never really set it in stone that we are dating, but I have a feeling if I asked, I'd be punished for another comment like that. It's more like an unspoken agreement, I'm his, and he's

mine.

FBGM Group Chat

Angelina: Almost there.

Gia: Us too, see you soon!

We pull up to Nico's club a few minutes later. As soon as

we got inside, I spotted Gia and Rosanna. With her loud voice

and bright energy, it's hard to miss Gia. I run up to them so fast I

have to hold my dress down from riding up and showing

everyone my ass. The girls lean into me and whisper so Nico

can't hear when the hug breaks up.

"Okay, introduce us to your dark, broody boyfriend

who's stolen you from us," Rosie whispers.

"Yeah, he better have a golden dick if he's the reason we

haven't seen you all week," Gia adds.

"GG!" Rosie and I yell at her, but she knows we're joking.

Gia never has a filter, and I love her for it. She is always herself, never faking or hiding her personality.

I look over to Nico, who is leaning against the bar with his hands in his pockets, eyeing me carefully. I signal him over, and he smiles at me and walks up to us three girls.

"Nico, I'd like you to meet Gia and Rosanna. I've been telling you about my best friends. Girls, meet Nicolai Leone," I say with one hand on his back and my head against his bicep.

"Ladies, it's a pleasure," Nico says politely with a nod.

Rosie's protective side cuts right to the chase. She's like the mom of the group, the responsible one.

"You treat her well?" she asks.

"Of course. Angelina deserves the best," he says while smiling at me.

Gia is much more friendly than Rosie when it comes to first impressions. Rosie will ease up once she knows Nico has good intentions with me.

"Nice to meet you, Nicolai!" Gia chirps.

Gia hugged Nico, and I warned him this would happen. She's a hugger. Gia is like a golden retriever, friendly and cute.

Nico just pats her on the shoulder, clearly uncomfortable by her boldness. He's not used to being hugged by strangers or anyone, for that matter.

"Yeah, you too," he says.

I look over at Nico and can tell he's a little stressed—not because of Gia but the club. He's looking all over the place like he's making a mental to-do list of things he needs to catch up on.

I lift on my toes and whisper in his ear, "Go. Take care of business. I'll be with Gia and Rosie all night anyway."

"Are you sure? I can stay with you and come back to work tomorrow or something."

"I don't mind. Plus, I'm sure the girls would love to gossip about you, and they can't do that with you eavesdropping," I advise him.

"Thanks, baby," he says. Then he kisses me on the forehead, and the girls gush over it.

"I'll watch the cameras and check on you now and then. If you need me, come to the office. Don't hesitate, okay? You come first," he says.

I roll my eyes at him. "You're procrastinating."

"Okay, okay. Have fun." He leans in toward my ear so no one but me can hear. "Not too much fun. I'll be watching, and if I see you do anything with another man, I won't hesitate to turn that ass the same shade as your lips."

My cheeks turn dark red, and I wish I could say it's from the heat in here, but Nico's words do it for me.

He walks away, and I'm standing here grinning like a lovestruck teenager.

Gia groans. "Ugh, I want a Nico in my life."

"You'll find one soon, Gia. I know you will. It'll come easy with your energy and looks," I reassure her.

She tilts her head and raises her eyebrows. "True. I mean, even I wouldn't be able to resist myself."

One thing about Gia is that I've never seen her sad. She's always bubbly and light, so I can't tell whether she's genuinely happy or hiding her sadness. She's had relationships in the past, but they've never worked out. Her exes claimed she was "too much" for them, and I wanted to cut their tongues out for saying that about such a kind-hearted person. One of these days, she will find a man who appreciates her personality as much as Rosie and I do.

"C'mon let's go take some shots," Gia says.

"Shots plural?"

"Yup, you heard me," she confirms.

I hate taking shots because of how fast they catch up to me, but I want to have fun with my girls, so I oblige.

"Three lemon drops, please" Gia orders from the bartender.

Rosie tries to decline the shot, but Gia convinces her to take at least one and sober up later. The bartender makes our shots and hands them to us, and I dread the sting coming that vodka leaves behind.

"To fuck bitches get money!" Gia yells carelessly.

"Woo!" We look to Rosie.

"Ugh, fine. To FBGM," she says as she raises her shot glass.

Rosie sounds miserable, but she secretly loves this, trust me. We shoot the shots and just as I expected, they burn going down my throat, but the lemon flavor is tasty. Gia signals the bartender for another round, and I almost stop her but decide against it. I'm having fun. One more can't hurt, right?

Wrong. We take about three more after that, and I am now so blackout drunk I'm wobbling. I have to pee so bad. I was trying not to break the seal, but my bladder won this argument. It's very loud on the dance floor, so I have to scream for the girls to hear me.

"I have to pee! I'll be right back!" I yell at the girls.

"We'll go with you!" Rosie yells over the loud music.

"No, it's okay. You two are having fun. It's just over there. I'll be quick."

I walk away—well, more like wobble away. I almost stopped in Nico's office, but I decided I couldn't wait a second longer to go pee.

I turn the corner to the bathrooms and walk down the hallway while holding onto the wall for support. The hallway is dark, but I can still see where I'm going. I find the women's room and pull on the handle, but I don't enter before someone grabs me from behind. A strong arm is draped across my body, preventing me from running away, and the other hand is over my mouth with a cloth. I thrash all I can. This man isn't Nico. He doesn't smell or feel like him, so I have no idea who's behind me. The defense attempts that Nico taught me in training are useless since I'm plastered and fucking up every move. It doesn't help my situation that the person grabbing me is much stronger than I am. The room gets darker, and my eyelids flutter shut. Next thing I know I'm met with darkness and silence.

CHAPTER 24

Nicolai

I have been stuck in the office all night and right as I'm about to leave to find Angelina, Rocco walks in.

"Hey, man! We need to talk," he says.

"Rocco, it's great to see you and all, but I have a very drunk girl out there that needs to be tended to," I say in a rush.

I go to stand, but Rocco stops me.

"You broke off your partnership with Enzo? Where does that leave us?"

I run a hand down my face. I knew this conversation was coming soon, but I was just hoping he would drop it or forget about our deal.

"Unfortunately, that deal included Enzo, so it's no longer valid," I tell him.

"You're kidding, right? I need that deal. You know I do," he says in a stressed voice.

"I know, but I can't uphold my end without Enzo. He could sue me for keeping the contract active, and I don't want to deal with the legal bullshit. Look, you can keep the money we gave you, and maybe sometime in the future, we can write up a new contract between you and me. Alright?" I ask, hoping we can end this conversation.

He nods his head. He doesn't seem pleased, but I can't deal with babying his feelings right now.

"I got to go. I'll call you," I say as I hold the door open for him to leave.

He nods and walks out the door. This gives me a chance to check on Angelina. I've been watching her on and off all night, and she took way too many shots. She was dancing and having fun with her friends whenever I checked the cameras, so

I continued catching up on work. I finally finished up and was ready to take her home when Rocco walked in and interrupted my plans. I look over at the cameras and see Gia and Rosanna dancing, but no Angelina. I scan my eyes all over the club but can't find her. I rewind the cameras to hopefully see where she headed off to. Five minutes ago, she was wobbling to the bathroom. She shouldn't have gone alone. I watch her find the bathroom and round the corner when someone in a black hoodie comes up from behind. I can tell by his build that it's a man. I can't see his face or where he even came in from. He covers her mouth with a laced cloth, and she passes out in his arms. He drags her out of the club, but I can't see where to; the cameras stop there.

I've never known fury like this. I thought I knew what anger felt like before, but I was so far off. This is on a whole other level. I'm angry at the fucker who took her and angry at myself for not protecting her. What happened to her coming first?

I want to kill everyone who walked through these doors in hopes that just one of them is that man. I punch the wall nearest to me and leave a hole in its wake. It doesn't help the pain I feel. My chest hurts, and it starts to get hard to breathe. I bend over with my hand on my heart and grab the desk for support. I start hyperventilating and doing everything I can not to think of the dark memory that's invading my thoughts.

Fifteen years ago

"I'm never gonna be as good as you!" I shouted at my papa.

"Buddy that's not true. You almost beat me that time," my papa said with pride.

"All I had was a pair, and you had a full house. Not even close," I whined.

My mamma walked into the living room where my papa and I were playing poker.

"Honey, give him a break. You guys have been at it for hours," my mamma said while messing with my hair.

"One of these days I'll win and make you proud," I said with determination.

"Oh, my sweet boy. We're already so proud of you."

My mamma kissed my cheek but was interrupted as someone knocked on the door. She looked at my papa and then at me.

"Go to your room and take a break, Nico. You guys can play later."

I ran to my room with the deck of cards and practiced on my bed. The poker king doesn't take breaks, and I wanted to be as good as my papa. I heard him talking to someone in the kitchen. The other voice doesn't sound like my mamma's. A few seconds later, she entered my room and rushed up to me.

"Hi, sweetie. Do you want to make Mamma and Papa even prouder?" she asked.

Why is her voice trembling? Why does she look so scared?

I nodded my head and brushed off my curious questions.

"Go hide in your closet. Don't make a sound or come out; I'll be the proudest mamma in the world. Can you do that for me?" she asked, hopeful.

"Yes, Mamma."

A tear ran down her cheek. My mamma is so pretty, even when she's crying.

"It's okay, Mamma. Don't be sad. I'll make you proud," I told her.

"I love you, my sweet boy," she said with a crack in her voice.

"I love you too, Mamma."

I ran over to my closet and hid inside, even though it was dark and scary. She shut the closet door and ran out of my room. I was met with pure silence for minutes—until I wasn't.

Pop.

Pop.

The sound was so loud I had to cover my ears. When it stopped, I took my hands off my ears and heard the front door close. Then, I was met with silence once again. My mamma said not to come out, but maybe the popping sound was a signal? I opened the closet door and quietly left my bedroom towards the living room.

"Mamma? Papa?" I call out.

When I round the corner, I let out a sound I'd never heard come out of my mouth before.

I rushed over to my mamma and papa, who were covered in red.

"Mamma, wake up!" I shook her, but she didn't move.

"Papa! Papa, please!" I cried.

"You can't leave me!"

"Please!"

"Please." I cried silently and lay with them both.

I didn't get any other screams out because I stopped breathing altogether. My chest hurt like it never had before, and my heart raced. I heard myself breathing, but it felt like I was running out of air. I counted up to ten, and it helped. I lay with my mamma and papa until I was pulled off of their bodies. Did I make you proud?

"Seven."

"Eight."

"Nine."

"Ten." I took one final deep breath and calmed.

I haven't had a panic attack for years. I managed to control it by counting, but I'm still spiraling. Where is she? Is she okay?

I walk out of my office and head to her friends. They're still dancing, oblivious to what just happened to Angelina.

"Nico! Get Angelina out of the bathroom. She's taking forever! Or did she lie to us and sneak off with you?" Gia asks.

Rosanna catches the pained look in my eyes and grabs Gia's arm to stop her from dancing.

"What is it?"

"Someone took Angelina by the bathroom. Was there anyone creeping you guys out tonight or anything out of the ordinary?"

"What do you mean someone took her?" Rosanna asks.

"I mean, they came up behind her, drugged her, and took her out of here," I clarify to the both of them.

Gia covers her mouth with her hand as tears well in her eyes. Rosanna remains calm, but I can tell she's worried and freaking out internally, just not showing it.

"Nothing was out of the ordinary. We were having a fun night. Angelina would have told me if someone was giving her the creeps," Rosanna says.

I run a hand through my hair. I'm aggravated with myself and her friends for not protecting her. I can't blame them, though; I know Angelina wouldn't want me to.

"Alright. I'll find her, I promise. You girls should go home. It's not safe," I advise.

"C'mon, Gia, I'm sober enough to drive us. Keep us updated, and call if you hear anything. I'll keep looking tonight, too," Rosanna says.

"No. You two get some sleep. There's nothing you can do that I haven't already thought of. I'll find her," I say with enough confidence that I hope they believe me.

"Okay." Rosanna gives in and walks Gia out as she cries in her arms.

I watch as they leave, making sure they go safely. I walk up to the usher and ask him for the night's guest list. I make a copy and go over it in my office. The only names I recognize are the girls, Rocco, and a few gamblers upstairs. They all know better than to cross me and are way too chicken and stupid to get away with it. Meaning that whoever took her is either a stranger or they snuck in.

"Mother fucker!" I yell.

God dammit, I'll find her. They don't know that it's the most hauntingly beautiful thing ever when a devil falls in love. And they should be terrified, for I will go to the depths of hell for her.

CHAPTER 25

Angelina

I open my eyes slowly. I'm disoriented and confused, and my head is throbbing. Even though I was kidnapped and could quite possibly die, I'm not scared. Nico taught me to be courageous, to be the one doing the scaring rather than the scared one.

It looks like I'm in a parking garage, but I can't tell for sure if that's where I am because it's so dark. I'm shivering from the cold concrete floor, and I feel sick. I don't know if I'm nauseous because of the alcohol, the situation I'm in, or whatever drugs they gave me.

I look up and see my father standing across from me, and that's what makes me end up vomiting all over the floor. I can't do anything right away to get away from him since my hands are tied behind my back on a pole. What feels like zip ties are cutting into my wrists, tied so tightly that I'm surely bleeding.

"Sorry about that. Can't have you running away, and we both know you would," my father says.

"You kidnapped me?! What the hell is wrong with you?" I shout.

"Where should I start? First, you think you can run off like I don't exist. You're own father," he scoffs. "Then you dare to ignore me and cut me out of your life. As if I didn't work my ass off to provide for you all these years. And then! Oh, get this! You fucking rob me of my partner and job!" He laughs as if this is funny to him.

"So, you kidnap me? How does fix anything!" I shout again.

"It fixes everything. Here, I can control you. Since you need a fatherly figure to keep you in check. Second, your being here will make it so easy to lure Nicolai. I can't wait to put a bullet through his head," he says, completely serious.

No.

"Leave him out of this."

My father bends his knees so he's eye level with me and lightly graces my cheek. I pull away as far as I can from his touch.

He tilts his head to the side. "It's sweet you think you can make demands. You will rot down here right beside Nico. Except he'll be dead, and you'll be miserable," he says with a chirpy voice, as if he can't wait.

He goes on. "I tried to give you a good life, Angelina, but you couldn't handle a little control. So, whose fault is it truly that you're in this predicament? Hm?"

"You tried to give me a good life? When? Was it when I got scolded any time I tried to leave the house? Or when you hit my mother for simply breathing? Oh wait, I know! It must have been when you slapped me across the face for getting the freedom I deserve! You're right; I was having the time of my life thanks to you," I finish sarcastically.

My father walks up to me slowly and then stops, standing above me. I meet his stare head-on and prepare for whatever comes next after that rampage I just had.

Just as I expected, I had something coming to me for my actions. He lifts his boot, reels his leg back, and kicks me in the stomach—hard. My body lies still on the concrete, in a fetal position, as he kicks me a second time. The harsh impact makes me cough and dry heave on the ground under me. *I am not weak. I will not surrender.*

"That's all you got, old man?" I ask, barely able to breathe.

"You're lucky I want you alive, or I'd kill you already. You will obey me, and never question or hesitate to do as I ask."

He bends down to my eye level, hands on his knees, and says, "Oh, how I missed walking my pup on a leash."

With that comment, I spit on his face. Maybe it was the wrong move, but how fucking dare he call me his pup. He closes his eyes, takes a deep breath, and stands. I almost think he will let it pass when he turns to walk away, but then he comes back full force and punches me in the face. Thankfully, my teeth stay intact, but that doesn't mean it didn't hurt. I taste copper and spit on the ground, covering the concrete in blood splatter.

His voice is clipped and angry. "You will learn to respect me. Pull a stunt like that again, and I won't be so kind."

That was kind?

He starts to walk away.

"I have to prepare for our friend to arrive, but I'll be around, so don't try anything stupid," he says.

He looks to the right at someone, but all I can see is a shadow.

He speaks to someone next to him. "Don't take your eyes off of her. If she tries to escape, do whatever you must. I don't give a shit what you do as long as you keep her alive."

As my father leaves the room, I try to get a better look at the shadow. I can tell it's a man based on their tall height and medium build, which is slightly terrifying, but I don't show him any hint of my fear. He gets closer to the light and that's when I recognize him.

He has black hair that almost covers his eyes and a barely noticeable tattoo under his dark locks. I don't know his name, but I do know I've seen him twice. Once, when he was staring at me and my friends that first day at the club and second from poker night. Based on their interactions, Nico knows this man well, but I don't know him at all.

"Nice to see a friendly face?" he asks. His voice is deep with a thick Italian accent. It sounds slightly younger and less intimidating than Nico's.

"Who are you?"

"Name's Rocco. We've met," he says.

"Yeah, I remember. Poker night."

"Yes, but that's not what I had in mind," he says.

He digs into his pockets, pulls out a set of keys, and then hits a button. A car turns on in the distance, and that's when it hits me. That was the car following me and Nico after dinner.

"You followed me?" I ask.

"Sure did. I did not expect to lose you so quickly. I must say, you are one hell of a driver," he says.

"Why are you helping him? Nico will kill you for this," I warn him.

"Enzo is my boss. Nicolai broke off our business deal, and I'll admit that made me very angry. Enzo came in and offered me another deal to help take you and get revenge on Nicolai. I mean, I couldn't pass that up. Can you blame me?" he asks as if I'd agree with him.

I need to find a way out of this. I don't know Rocco at all, but I know my father, and there is no reasoning or convincing him. My only way out is Rocco. He sits down a bit away from me and lights a cigarette.

I close my eyes and think back to that first night I met Nico. I remember my surroundings, a few faces, and the loud sounds of music, laughter, and conversation. I try to focus on the memory so much so that it feels like reality. I remember the exact moment I spotted Nicolai above me. A lot of eyes were on me, but not like his. His dark eyes seared into my soul, and I couldn't look away even if I tried. He was attractive and rich and everything I was looking for that night. While a big part of me thought I could fool him and get away with it, another small part of me knew there was no fooling someone like him. Yet I still stole from him, hoping he'd catch me in the crime, curious of what he would do to me for it. *I miss him.*

When I looked up and saw Nicolai, he wasn't the only one staring. For a split second that night, my eyes glanced at the man Nico was speaking to, and that man was Rocco. Except Rocco wasn't staring at me. He was staring at Rosanna the same way Nico looked at me. With want, with feral need. *Bingo.*

Now, I won't sell my friend, but I will use her as leverage, as manipulation.

"That night at the club, you were staring at my friend."

He pulls the cigarette from his mouth and releases a breath of smoke. He looks over to me and makes eye contact. I can tell I have caught his interest, but he looks away and tries to brush it off.

"Yeah, and? I stare at a lot of women," he claims.

I carefully choose my next words and whisper, ensuring my father can't eavesdrop.

"You help me save Nico, and I'll give you her name," I whisper.

I am not lying; I will give it to him. What he doesn't know is that I'll never let him get near her.

He laughs. "That's not enough."

Negotiation. I can do that.

"Did Enzo tell you who Nico's new partner is?"

"No. Wouldn't be surprised if he was going solo," he says.

"I'm his partner. I'll give you her name and reconcile your old deal. You won't work with Nico; you'll work with me. Same benefits, and a contract. There will be no breaking it, or you have my permission to put a bullet in my head," I say honestly.

Maybe this is naive of me, but do I have another choice?

He drops the cigarette, steps on it, and approaches me. He pulls a gun out from behind him, and I regret everything I just said. I am going to die. Of course, he's loyal to my father. Everyone who isn't Nico or me is.

"Tell me you're not lying. If I think you are, I will not hesitate to shoot."

I truly am not lying to Rocco. Every part of this deal is legit. I look into his eyes and pray to God he believes me.

"You have my word," I say without blinking, breathing, or breaking his eye contact.

He stares back, and I can feel him reading my thoughts. Please believe me, please believe me.

He lowers his gun and puts it back in his pants. I release the breath I was holding onto.

"We have a deal. Now tell me her name, and I'll free your hands."

"Rosanna Mariano," I answer truthfully.

He looks at me with his hands on his hips. "A Mariano, huh?"

"Yeah," I smirk, "good luck with that."

The Mariano's have a pristine reputation. They expect so much from Rosanna, so I know they won't welcome a man like Rocco into their lives.

He cuts off my zip ties, and I feel like I can finally take a deep breath. Those were killing me.

"Here's what's going to happen. You will listen and do everything I say because if you don't, none of us will walk out of here alive."

CHAPTER 26

Nicolai

I am going to fucking kill everyone until someone breaks about where she is. I don't care if no one is left.

I'm speeding down the road to Enzo's house. I would not put it past him to be involved in this. When I arrive, I run up to the door and pound on it. A few moments later, Mrs. Vittori answers, and when she does, I can't help but stare. She has a black eye, finger bruises on her arms, and a red handprint on her cheek.

"What happened to you?" I ask.

"Oh, these?" She waves her hand in the air, brushing it off. "I can be a little clumsy sometimes."

She's the worst liar I've ever met, and it makes me wonder how her daughter is one of the best liars I've ever met.

"Have you seen Angelina?" I ask.

"No. I thought she was with you. That's what she told me a few days ago," she says.

"She was. Then I lost her. What about Enzo? Where is he?" I ask.

"I honestly don't know. He's always out. I don't ask where he goes since he doesn't like me in his business," she says. I'm not surprised. Like I said, Enzo is a very private man.

"Mind if I come in and look around?"

"Of course. I'll stay by the door and let you know if my husband arrives. He wouldn't be happy about you snooping, but it can be our little secret," she says.

"Thank you, Mrs. Vittori. I'll find her, I promise. I know you two don't have the best mother-daughter relationship, but I can tell you love her, and she loves you," I say, hoping to bring her some sense of comfort.

She offers me a faint smile, and it's nice to see. I've never seen her smile.

I search every room in this house—the master, office, garage, even Angelina's—but don't find anything that helps. I don't know if the kidnapping has anything to do with Enzo, but my gut tells me it does. I leave and head back to the club. There are a few people I need to have a not-so-friendly chat with.

Less than thirty minutes later, I arrived. While I was on the way, I called my employees and told them what to do. I entered my office, took a seat, put my feet on my desk, and waited.

Shortly after, my employees enter with two of Enzo's men.

"Shut the door."

I pull out my gun and cock it.

"Either one of you opens your mouth about where Enzo is, or I'll open it for you," I say, my tone vicious.

I dangle my gun in the air as a threat and grin. They're both sweating and shaking. *Amateurs*. They stand there in silence. When I stand, one of them speaks up.

"I don't know, I swear!"

"That's not good enough," I say.

I shove the gun in his mouth and shoot without hesitation. I don't have time to waste. I turn to the guy to my right.

"Your turn," I order and raise my gun.

"Wait. Wait!" He puts his hands up to stop me. "I don't know where he is, but I know who might."

"Keep talking," I say.

"Enzo recently made a deal with Rocco Accardi. They've been together ever since. There's no way he doesn't know where he is," he confesses.

Rocco fucking Accardi. That bastard was distracting me while she was kidnapped. Coincidence? I don't believe in those.

I shoot this guy, too, just for the hell of it.

After my employees take care of the bodies, I catch something on the cameras. Rocco walks in with some blonde girl on his hip as if everything's normal and dandy.

I walk out of my office and toward the VIP lounge, where he's seated. I enter the room, and the bastard dares to greet me.

"Nico! Care for a game?" he asks, pointing at the poker table.

I walk up to him and remain as calm and collected as I can be when, really, on the inside, my blood is boiling. I stand in front of him so no one can see my front but him, lean down and push the gun against his cock.

I stand to his side so no one else can hear my threat. "Tell me where she is, or I swear to God I will shoot your dick off."

He puts his hands up in surrender. "Chill the fuck out, dude; I'll take you to her. But if you kill me, she'll die too. I have people watching, waiting for a signal," he warns.

Bummer. I would have enjoyed watching him bleed.

I put my gun away, and he eases up.

"Didn't think to check your own club's parking garage Nicolai, did you?" he asks.

Mother. Fucker.

I run out of the club toward the garage. She has to be alive; hell will break loose if she's not.

CHAPTER 27

Angelina

Rocco comes back, and he's out of breath. My father's back is to me as he speaks, and that's when I sneak up behind him. He talks to Rocco, thinking his plan is going along as it should. He has zero clue.

"Nico's on his way now," Rocco informed him.

"Good. Hear that, Angelina? I hope you're ready to say your goodbyes," he shouts, thinking I'm farther away than I am.

He turns around to face me but stops moving when I press the gun to his forehead. Rocco stands there and does nothing to stop me. I mean, why would he? He's the one who gave me the gun. He walks up to my father while I hold the gun on him and removes the gun from inside my father's jacket.

"Goodbyes to Nico or you, father?" I ask.

His eyes look over to Rocco, but he doesn't dare move his head.

"What have you done?" he asks Rocco and is very pissed off, might I add. He is seething but can't do anything about it.

Rocco shrugs. "If someone offers a better deal, of course, I'm going to take it."

"Then she lied!" My father shouts. "She's a nobody. She probably doesn't even know how to shoot a damn gun. She's as worthless as her mother."

Does he have a death wish?

I smile when I see Nico walking in from behind my father. God, it's good to see him. Right now is not the time for catch-up, though.

Nico speaks up. "That's where you're wrong, Enzo. Angelina is better than me, Rocco, and way better than you'll ever be. You have always underestimated her, and that'll be your downfall."

"Fine. Go ahead, shoot me. You'll never find out what happened to your parents," my father says, catching us all off guard.

I considered many scenarios for how this interaction could go, but the mention of Nico's parents was not one of them.

"Don't listen to him, Nico. He's lying," I say.

My father shakes his head and says, "Believe whatever you want. I know you've been looking for them for years and have no leads. I'm all you've got."

Nico pulls out his gun, so now my father has one on the back of his head and the front. He's surrounded.

"Tell me the name, or you're dead." Nico's voice comes out pained with a hint of desperation.

My father smiles and breaks out in a laugh. "I'm already dead. I'm not stupid. I know there's no walking out of here alive. I raised you in the mafia world Nicolai. Made you into the man you are. Based on that, I know you will not show an ounce of mercy."

Nico shakes his gun in the air. "Who fucking killed my parents!?"

I've never heard Nico shout like this, and the tears welling up in his eyes are breaking my heart.

"Enzo Vittori," my father says, with an evil smile.

I gasp, Nico stops breathing, and I see Rocco's shock. He didn't know. None of us did.

Nico's voice cracks. "No. They were your friends, that doesn't make any sense. All those years of helping me find their killer when the whole time you were steering me away from you!"

My father shrugs. "What can I say? They kept embarrassing me in front of everyone. I owed them a lot of money in poker, and they thought they could threaten me because of it. I couldn't allow it. I'm sure you understand."

A tear drops from Nico's eyes. He turns to look into mine, and I can tell he's asking my permission. I nod my head without hesitation. I feel no sympathy or love for my father, not after all of this. He kidnapped me, mentally and physically abused me, and killed Nico's only family. I can never forgive him for the excruciating pain he has caused me, Nico, or my mother, that we will carry with us forever. The sliver of heart I had left for my father has now disintegrated into ash.

Nico doesn't get the chance to shoot because a gunshot rings in the air from another direction.

I have to cover my ears from the loud sound. All I hear is ringing and faint shouting but I can't make out what's being said. I think I'm shouting Nico's name, but I can't hear my voice.

When I open my eyes, I see my father dead on the ground. That's not the sad part, though. The sad part is that I feel nothing. I don't cry at the sight of his lifeless body like a normal daughter would. We didn't have what most would call a father-daughter relationship.

Nico runs to me and assesses me from my face, chest, and legs with worry in his expression.

"Are you okay? Are you hurt?" he asks.

"I'm okay. Nico, who killed him?" I reply.

Before he can answer, a voice from in the shadows speaks up.

"I did," a female voice says.

"That was single-handedly the hottest thing I've seen in my life," Rocco says.

I ignore Rocco's comment and look back to the voice I recognize.

"Rosie? How did you—? What are you doing here?" I ask, my voice full of surprise and concern.

She rushes up to me and hugs me.

"I'm so sorry. I know he was your father, but I couldn't just stand by while he kidnapped you and killed so many innocent people," she says.

"How did you know where we were?" I ask.

"I followed Nico here. Then I snuck in behind him. When I saw all the blood on the ground and what your father had done to you I couldn't stop myself from pulling the trigger," she says.

"How do you even know how to use a gun? And aim so well?" I ask, the questions continuously pouring out of me.

She motions me to the side, away from everyone for privacy.

She whispers, "If I tell you something, you can't tell anyone unless you trust them with your life and mine."

"Okay, you're scaring me," I say.

"I heard through the vine that you're Nico's new partner, which got you into this mess. Well, I'm sort of in this mess, too," she says with a chuckle.

She goes on. "I'm a spy in the mafia. So is Gia. She mainly just helps with cover-ups and small shit. She's still getting used to the crime, but she likes the money in the business."

I shake my head. "No. There's no way. What about your family? They would never approve of this."

"You're right; they wouldn't. Hence, why I'm a spy, and nobody knows. I make my money exposing secrets. People don't know about me, so when I'm around the higher-ups, they run their mouths without thinking twice," she says.

I take the time to process her words. "Wow. I don't know if I love or hate this lifestyle for you."

"Then let me ask you this. Do you like this lifestyle for yourself?"

I answer truthfully. "Yes. I've never felt stronger as a woman in a career full of men."

"That's exactly how I feel and why I started in the first place," she says.

Maybe this is a good thing.

An idea dawns on me. "Oh my god! All three of us have to work together. Could you imagine the shit we could do?!"

Rosie giggles at the thought. "I would love that. We have to talk to Gia first, though. We can do all that later. Right now, go get your man. He hasn't stopped staring at you, and he probably lip-read our whole convo knowing his psychotic ass."

"Hey, he's my psycho. And Rosie? Thank you," I say.

She hugs me and leaves the parking garage. As I make my way over to Nico, I realize he's looking around for something, or rather someone.

"Angelina. Where's Rocco?" he asks.

"I'm not sure, but you have to let him go. We have a business contract, and if you touch him, he can kill me," I tell him.

"Are you kidding? I hope you're kidding because there is no fucking way I am letting that man live after tying you up and hurting you," he says.

"He didn't tie me up. That was my father. And he never laid a hand on me. He helped me. Whose gun do you think I was holding?" I ask sarcastically. He knows the answer.

His jaw twitches. He looks furious with me, but I can tell he's contemplating his actions regarding Rocco.

"Fine. Just because I won't kill him doesn't mean I don't want to. I don't like him one bit."

"That's okay. I didn't expect you two to be besties. Oh, by the way, we have more friends in the business. I'll give you all the details later. Right now, I just want to make up for the lost time away from my psychotic boyfriend."

EPILOGUE

Angelina

I'm standing in the kitchen of my new bakery, *Cupcake Heaven*, decorating the strawberry cupcakes I baked with my mom when I hear the bells jingle from the door opening. Nico approaches me, and I take the chance to smear pink icing on his nose. He wipes it off and puts his finger into his mouth.

"Delicious," he says.

He leans in and whispers in my ear so my mom can't hear. "I'd rather have a taste of you."

He grabs a few of our messy dishes and puts them in the sink. Then he rolls the long sleeves of his button-up and starts hand washing them. He does this often, coming in his free time to help me out with my business, as if buying me a building wasn't helpful enough.

As soon as my mom catches him cleaning, she objects.

"No, no. You are not cleaning up our mess."

"Mrs. Vittori, I really don't mind. Please, I'd love to help," Nico says.

"You know better than to call me that. Please, call me Tori," my mother says.

It's been months since my father's death, and life has been so peaceful and full of joy. Shortly after he passed, my mom came out of her shell and opened up to me. We talked, cried, laughed, yelled a little, and cried some more. She felt terrible for not being a better mother to me growing up, but I understood why she couldn't with my father's control and abuse preventing her love. We made up, and now we're closer than ever.

Even she and Nico have gotten close. She's almost been like a mother figure to him, in a non-weird way, if that makes sense. Seeing them together has warmed my heart, and I can see how happy Nico is. We are a family now, and I couldn't ask for more. She works with me in the bakery and spends her free time doing just about everything. She's been having fun experimenting, considering she couldn't do anything with my father around. She's thriving in the freedom just as I am.

Nico's business has boomed with me as his partner and everyone else we've added. Gia and Rosie are now my partners; unfortunately, Rocco is too. Rosie keeps an eye on high-up mafia men and lets me know if there are any whispers I should know about. Gia has been surprisingly helpful. She's all sunshine and rainbows but can somehow handle covering up bodies to look less like murder and more like accidents. I won't lie when I say I've enjoyed taking down people who deserve their doomed fate.

Rosie heard rumors about three mysterious girls who joined the mafia known as Whispers of Vice and Virtue. Most of the men aren't happy about us women holding so much power, but they're too scared to do anything to stop us. It's public knowledge that I'm Nico's partner and a part of this criminal association, but no one knows I'm one of the Whispers of Vice and Virtue. We girls came up with the name after we agreed to work together in secret. Rosie is Whispers, I am Vice, and Gia is Virtue. It suits us well, and I am so proud of the life us girls have made for ourselves.

I finish icing the cupcake in my hand and turn around to grab another. I stop in my tracks, and the cupcake I was holding plops on the floor. Nico is on one knee, and I look over to my mom, who has tears in her eyes and a big smile on her face.

I look back down at Nico, who is holding a box. He opens it to reveal a large, red diamond. It's beautiful and perfect and takes my breath away.

"Angelina, from the moment I saw you that night in the club I knew you were it for me. You're stubborn, badass, and so fucking beautiful it hurts to look at you sometimes. The day that I lost you was the scariest day of my life, and I've seen some scary shit. I won't lose you again, and that's a promise to both you and Tori. I'll never stop trying to make you happy, mio dolce angelo. I know this isn't a grand proposal, and you deserve more, but I couldn't wait a second longer. Te amo, Angelina, con tutto il cuore. Will you marry me? I won't take no for an answer, but I promised your mom I'd ask."

I'm sobbing so hard that I forget to answer him.

"Yes! Oh my god, yes!" I yell.

He kisses me, then slides the ring on my finger. A perfect fit.

"It's so beautiful," I cry.

My mom starts jumping up and down while crying.

"We're going to have so much fun planning the wedding! Nico, welcome to the family. I wouldn't accept anyone else for my daughter," my mother says.

Seeing those two hugging makes me cry even harder than I was. I am so over-the-top happy, and my heart is full.

I can't wait to spend the rest of my life with Nico, even if that means selling my soul to the devil.

Stay tuned for Rocco and Rosanna's story next...